WINDLYN VALE

TOBIAS YOUNGBLOOD

RIPOSTE

JOIN THE YOUNGBLOOD NEWSLETTER

Members get free books, exclusive content, and first look at upcoming releases.

See the back of the book for details on how to join.

Contents

1.	Funeral	1
2.	Siv's Trap	7
3.	Mist	14
4.	Roast	22
5.	Red Tide	27
6.	Rayla	32
7.	Atul the Selfless	37
8.	The Cliffs of Glimryn Forest	40
9.	Tempest	49
10.	The Blood Business	57
11.	Safe Keeping	75
12.	Unwelcome	80
13.	A Burrow Above	88
14.	Jaerwin	98
15.	The Watcher	106
16.	First Contact	114
17.	Master Yuryk	119
18.	Atul the Apprehensive	123
19.	Strigo the Stalwart	126
20.	Atul the Fearless	132
21.	Awake	138
22.	Bogged Down	144
23.	Battle of the Vale	147
24.	Sole Survivor	150
25.	Intruder	156
26.	Laguznal	161
27.	Escape	167
28.	Ships	172
	Epilogue	176

THE STORY CONTINUES...   179
Acknowledgments   181
About the Author   183

Copyright

Copyright © 2022 by Tobias Youngblood

The moral right of Tobias Youngblood to be identified as the author of this work has been asserted by him in accordance with the Copyright, Design and Patent Act 1988.

All events and characters in this book are fictitious, and any resemblance to actual persons or events is purely coincidental.

All rights reserved.

No part of this book may be reproduced in any form or by any electronic or mechanical means, including information storage and retrieval systems, without written permission from the author, except for the use of brief quotations in a book review.

Cover art © Vivid Covers | www.VividCovers.com

Map by Tobias Youngblood

Riposte Press

ISBN: 978-1-959649-01-4 (Print)

For my father, the selfless provider.
For my brother, lost too soon.

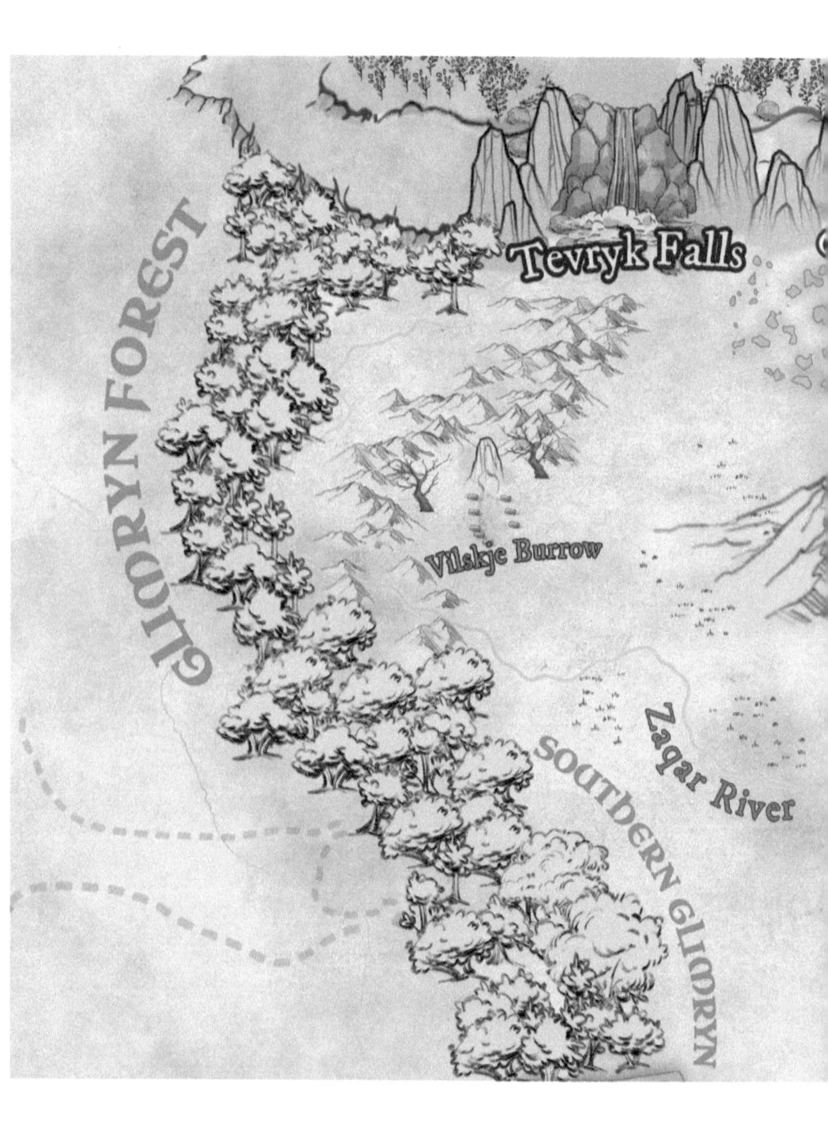

GLIDRYN FOREST
Tevryk Falls
Vilskje Burrow
Zaqar River
SOUTHERN GLIDRYN

iggen
Mt Svernos
WINDLYN VALE
Holidae Cove
The Spyrul Sea

FUNERAL

S iv watched as the vilskje glanced around the room, their beady eyes laden with worry. Their mantid bodies shuffled about on the shiny white stone. The Council Chamber was packed full—all of the council bloodline was in attendance as well as favorites of common creation. Outside in the drizzling rain, the remaining hundreds of the clan attended a second, more rudimentary funeral. No place inside could hold the entire clan at large.

To Siv's left, Master Wern stood on an elevated platform facing the clan. Large torches burned at the corners of the room and hollows in the rock above vented the smoke outside. A giant statue of the Father of Light stood at the center of the room watching over their proceedings, a posture which garnered the deity a secondary name of the Watcher.

As master, Wern was in command of the clan, though he relied on Siv for many of the hard decisions. Today was no exception.

Wern raised his arms to the crowd. "Fellow vilskje. We

gather today under sad circumstances. One of our own, a youth of less than two hundred years, has perished. Perillia was in the prime phase of learning when her studies, and indeed her life, were cut short. It brings me no joy to recount what has transpired, and yet, hear it we must." Wern turned and nodded to a vilskje of common creation. "Rufin, please tell us what transpired. Give us a direct account."

Rufin stood nervously and looked around. He lowered his head to Wern, a jerking shake of a nod. His thin lipless mouth turned down slightly at the corners. "Y-yes, Master. It was early. Just the two of us. We were down by Southern Glimryn Forest—not *in* the forest, but near the edge— picking herbs, when it came. Perillia had just learned her lark form the week before and I was helping her improve. The beast came from nowhere, and... more were behind it, near the forest, and... and..."

"Calm yourself, Rufin. You're in no danger here," said Wern. "What did you see?"

The youth swallowed and nodded. "At first I thought it was a grey wolf, but it was huge with a red stripe down its back. It growled and was on us... so fast." The sacs at the corners of his eyes expanded, filling with tear fluid. "We were just as we are now, in nakken-form. Perillia tried to shift to her lark and fly away, but she was too slow. Unskilled. She was at full-size still and covered in feathers when the beast clamped down on her throat and started shaking her. Then the others came in, howling, eyes wild. I took to the sky and was nearly swatted down, but somehow I managed to escape. Oh, maybe if I had worked with her more, she could have gotten away!" One of the sacs burst, splattering clear fluid to the floor. His voice turned to a whisper. "I can still hear her screams. She was my friend. I... wanted to help, but what could I do?"

Wern gestured to the clan's chief protector, Yuryk, to comfort Rufin.

Yuryk placed a clawed hand on Rufin's shoulder in a rare show of compassion. "This is not your fault, Rufin. There's nothing you could have done."

Wern turned to Siv. "Seer, have you identified these predators?"

Siv nodded. "Yes. The size, ferocity, the red stripe... these are dire wolves, Master. The Great Tome describes them in detail. And they still prowl Windlyn Vale."

Among the crowd, whispers grew into murmurs. The vilskje shuffled restlessly, their insectile bodies rustling like dry leaves.

"Quiet, everyone!" boomed Yuryk, and the room fell silent. The chief protector nodded to Wern.

Wern opened his hands to the crowd, the six clawed digits on each one extending outward like short spears. "This is the saddest of days, but I bring good news as well. Our scouts recovered enough of the body to qualify Perillia for Renewal. The Father of Light has accepted her back into the cycle. Even in her decimated state. Such is his love."

Siv looked up at the Father of Light, and a warmth spread through his breast and into his heart. The young vilskje would live again. The Watcher had embraced her, absorbing her body back into the soil at the Sacred Chamber deep within the burrow. It was a place only the master was permitted to tread. Now, her death was merely a short-term suffering.

He turned his gaze down to his own thorax, and his sadness returned. The sorrow was not for himself, for he did not know Perillia well, but for the girl's loved ones. He grazed a claw down one of his arms, thinking.

Blessed as it is, the promise of Renewal is never quite enough to recompense the living.

"I laid her to rest in the sacred ground," Wern continued, snapping Siv from his daydream. "When the time is right, she will claw her way to the surface once more, as she did only two short centuries ago."

The vilskje murmured approval, nodding their heads, their eyes a shade lighter in the reflected torchlight. "Praise the Watcher," said one. Others repeated the phrase.

"We must not fear these intruders, friends," continued Wern. "Siv has seen our clan through flood and famine. Even in our darkest hour, the seer carries the staunchest of torches."

All too often, Wern showered praise on Siv before dumping his problems onto him. Normally, Siv shouldered this burden with grace, but he hadn't been feeling like himself of late.

Not since the red tide.

It had washed up from the Spyrul Sea onto the shores of Windlyn Vale five days ago. The Great Tome called it an ill omen and, so far, Siv agreed. The next day, the dire wolves showed in their homeland for the first time. The day after that, Perillia had been killed.

In the crowd, a vilskje moved enough to pull Siv's gaze to her, where they locked eyes. Siv recognized Ilyana, and she lowered her head in a show of support, drawing his smile. The two had always shared an understanding, despite her common blood. Her unwavering support reminded him of something important—he had a plan.

Wern closed his hands into a fist. "As he has in the past, the seer will deliver us from this crisis." He turned to Siv. "Tell us, Seer, what wisdom do you impart? Will you guide the clan once more?"

Siv turned to face Wern. "Yes. Of course, Master." He pivoted to the crowd. "I am no better than any in this room, or those outside. I am merely a conduit for the Father of Light. It is he whom I ask for guidance. It is his wisdom I share. We must gather now in prayer for the Watcher's blessing. Have faith so we may become an entire clan of seers."

Siv lifted his arms toward the statue and shifted his weight to his hind legs so that he could rise to near Wern's height. "Assemble."

With those words, the clan took to their feet and formed a ring around the Father of Light, claw-in-claw. They started with a tight circle, and a greater ring surrounded that one, and so on until every vilskje from the audience joined in, like rings in a tree. Siv's eyes rolled back inside his head, and the center ring rotated as the vilskje recited the prayer:

"Oh, Father of Light, your grace flows like the falls. Allow us to serve you as a river serves the sea. You pulled us from the darkness of earth to emerge in your brilliance. You spared us from the Calamity. Now, bless us with your guidance, for we listen."

The vilskje repeated the last three words, "for we listen," until, eventually, it fell to a whisper and ceased. They unclasped hands and sat in silence, eyes turning back to Siv.

Siv returned to four legs, the six digits on each of his hands twitching at his sides like a cicada's wings. His pupils rolled forward to face the crowd once more. The clan's prayer had spawned an ecstatic heat inside of him. All doubts had been erased. The Watcher was with him.

His eyes fell upon Atul, the youth who would one day succeed him. "Stand, Atul," he said. Vilskje eyes turned to the youth.

Atul stood at once, nodding to his mentor. "I am ready, Seer."

Siv addressed the room at large. "The Father of Light has answered. Do you not feel the strength of his blessing? We shall fear these dire wolves no longer."

The crowd was silent aside from a few murmurs. They leaned closer, waiting for the seer's words.

"On the morrow, Atul and I will drive the dire wolves from Windlyn Vale."

Mouths fell open and eyes widened. Atul, on the other hand, smiled at Siv with adoring eyes. With a quick glance, he had accepted the task.

Yuryk voiced what the crowd would not. "How?"

Siv turned to the chief protector, confident, his insides still warm.

"I have a plan."

Siv's Trap

Atul limped up the snowy mountain pass. He turned his stag's head back, eyes wide, to find the dire wolves. He had spotted them a few minutes before. Broader than the common grey wolves which ventured from the woods at the edge of Windlyn Vale, the dire wolves were nearly twice the size, with fierce red eyes and a matching stripe of fur down the center of their backs.

The wolves converged on the mountain pass behind him, hunching low, stalking, their mouths open. Atul pretended not to see them, though his heart pounded. He leapt on stag hooves around a rocky bend, twisting up the side of Mount Svernos, briefly out of view of the pursuing pack. Off in the distance the Spyrul Sea churned with unrest, and the breadth of the valley unfolded, its beauty not as captivating under current circumstances. Disparate shapes in the vale below were at leisure, animals or his own kind, while his own life was at stake.

He didn't mind. He had chosen this.

Atul pulled his front hooves from a patch of snow and a

gale blew from the sea, pressing him into the mountain's side. The wind stalled his progress, and the thought of the pack gaining on him sent chills down his spine. He stepped forward on the narrow path and braced for more wind.

There was a snarling from behind, and Atul turned his head to see a massive dire wolf now at the head of the pack. It was nearly a foot taller than the others, its chest broad and its eyes bright. It stalked closer, snarling, drool dripping from its maw.

Atul jerked his head away and leapt up the cliff-side path, flicking the bloody gash on his stag's thigh with its tail, as if to comfort himself before the inevitable bloody end. Balancing his hooves precariously over loose stones, he gained distance from the dire wolves. The leader growled and Atul glanced back as the others joined in. The massive dire wolf stepped carefully over the thinning path, balancing the demands of its appetite with its need to survive.

Atul fled, placing one hoof in front of the other with practiced precision along the narrow pass. Ahead, the path widened, shrubs sprouted on the mountain cliff side, and a blue thrush perched on a small, wiry tree jutting from the side of the mountain.

If I can just make it there...

Another growl, closer this time, drove Atul to skip dangerously across the final stretch of the pass and leap onto the higher, more stable ground. Adrenaline surged through his body, and he bolted up the slope, quick despite his limp. He was grateful for the vegetation and boulders which sprang up around him along the way, grateful for any object that stood between himself and these dire wolves.

Their panting grew close until, at last, the rock wall to his left fell and he stumbled up the last bend, panting. The summit lay just ahead—a vast stone slab with sparse shrubbery jutting from random cracks in its surface. A stretch of tall bushes bordered the furthest edge of the summit. At this elevation, snow lay in sheets upon the path. Atul nearly fell on the uneven slope, a fatal mistake with the wolves so close.

Nearly there, if I can just...

Atul leapt to the summit as the wolf sprang at him from behind, narrowly missing his flank. The stag's back hoof cracked it in the jaw, drawing a howl of rage from the beast. In its fury, the wolf lost its footing on the snowy pass, sliding back down to the rest of the pack.

Atul limped across to the far edge of the summit, overlooking the vale and the sea to the east. He had made it, but there was nowhere to go from here. If Siv's plan didn't go as devised, the wolves would devour him. But he could still escape. There was still time.

No. Only a coward would flee now. Worse, I'd lose Siv's respect.

He turned back, his heart pounding in his ears. The entire pack was at the summit now, savoring a moment of victory before the meal. The leader stalked forward, slowly. The red stripe on its back stood erect, slicing toward the sky like a bloody blade. Its eyes glowed a bright scarlet. The dire wolf paused a few feet away, crouched low to the ground, and pointed its snout to the sky. It howled, and the pack joined in with their own shrieks—terrible, ghostly sounds.

Atul found himself playing the role of a prey animal too well. The stag's fear of death penetrated his vilskje heart, and for a moment he was paralyzed by the size and ferocity of the pack before him. These new predators had emerged from Glimryn Forest a few days ago. Siv claimed they'd never been here before. Atul had certainly never seen them.

Where could they have come from?

The wolves finished howling and the leader strode to the edge of the boulder, teeth bared. The others stood back, watching, allowing their leader the glory of the kill. The dire wolf's heavy breath steamed in the cold air.

One slip-up and I'm dead.

He nearly panicked in that moment, but he calmed himself, focusing on Siv's plan. He was nearly there. This had to work. Siv was the wisest of them.

After this, I'll be a hero.

He relied on his instincts, waiting for the moment the massive wolf would pounce. He spun and leapt once for the edge of the boulder and then again, off the summit and into the icy wind which swirled atop Mount Svernos. From the corner of his eye, he saw a blur of dark grey and red fur as the great wolf leapt, too late, after him, stopping just at the cliff's edge.

Wings sprouted from the stag's flesh, its body shrank and stretched and morphed in the air as it fell, rapidly sprouting feathers where deer hide had been, melting hooves and forming talons until in a matter of three seconds it appeared as a great hawk. Atul spread his wings into a six-foot span and turned his body up to catch the wind just in time to save himself from the rock spires just below. He opened his beak and inhaled until his lungs were full of the cool mountain air, cleansing him of the fear that had coursed through his body since he'd first spotted the dire wolves on the pass.

Atul flew skyward until he was high above the mountain. He turned back and saw that the wolves all stood near the edge of the summit now. They glared up at him in surprise and anger, snarling.

It's now or never.

Atul turned downward and dove straight at the pack leader. The wolf bent low on its haunches, its snarling maw turning up. At six feet away, Atul spun left.

The wolf lunged up, swiping at the hawk, its jaws wide. It missed narrowly to the left, and Atul swerved to slam the full force of his hawk body into the wolf's flank in the direction of the cliff's edge. Such was the great hawk's momentum that the force of impact drove the wolf over the edge. Atul speared his talons into the wolf's flesh and pushed off, separating himself enough to spread his wings and take to the sky once more, unharmed from the attack.

The dire wolf scrambled in the air, spinning and reaching for the edge of the cliff with a desperate howl, but it only got one claw over the lip. It plummeted, shrieking, pulled down by its own considerable weight. The rocky spires sliced through the dire wolf's flesh, impaling it on the mountainside in a gruesome display. Its crimson blood gushed over the rocks and its howls turned to exhausted, pathetic moans.

Then it was silent.

Atul circled back in the air, his wings spread to their full span, his heart racing with excitement. Below, the pack stood silent and still. In shock. Eventually, they began snarling and moving around again, but they were uncoordinated. Directionless without their leader.

Atul dove at another wolf, which stood a little separated from the rest at the southern edge of the summit. The wolf spun to avoid the hawk, not even daring to strike out. It teetered near the edge before moving safely inside, but the attack frightened it enough for it to flee the summit, back down the mountain slope, abandoning the pack. The rest of the wolves gave a wide berth to Atul's attack, backing away, unsure of what to do.

A bush at one side of the summit shook. From the thicket, a giant boar emerged, its lance-like tusks gleaming in the sunlight. It squealed and scraped its hooves on the frozen ground before charging at the largest of the remaining wolves in a berserk rage, its head down, giant curled tusks ready to impale.

Above, Atul screamed and dove at yet another wolf.

With Siv and Atul working together, the ambush proved too much for the shocked wolves. The pack scampered down the slope, howling in shame, tripping over each other in their haste to flee the mountain.

Once they were gone, Atul flew down and landed beside Siv at the center of the summit. The two nakken-shifted from hawk and boar into their natural form—the lanky, insectile bodies of the vilskje.

Siv turned to his young companion. He wiped at the mostly dried blood on Atul's thigh, a self-inflicted wound made for the trap. "You should not have struck that third time."

Atul turned to the seer, surprised by the criticism.

"But, Siv... I could sense their fear, and—"

"That wasn't part of the plan. It was an unnecessary risk." Siv cut him off. "My charge alone would have sent them reeling."

Atul's body felt hot. Feelings of anger and shame stirred inside. How had his moment of glory turned to reprimand? He bent the joints of his six appendages, lowering to a position just above the ground—a posture of frustration. He said nothing.

Siv scanned Atul over with his tiny eyes, and his stance softened. "Even without their leader, these dire wolves are deadly, Atul."

The seer crawled to Atul on four, like the walking-stick insects of Tevryk Falls. His two anterior limbs swung at his sides as he went. He placed one claw on the younger shifter's shoulder, giving it a small squeeze.

"Still," Siv said, allowing his thin, lipless mouth to turn up at the corners. "Your courage shines like a brilliant light over Windlyn Vale. Surely, Master Wern will smile upon you when we return."

Atul's posture lifted and he smiled.

"Thank you, Siv."

MIST

The sun's rays licked Siv's pale skin, blessing him with renewed energy. It had been a long wait at the summit as his feral boar, the most taxing of his dyr-forms—those shapes that mimic the animals of the world.

He walked to the edge of the summit and looked down. The limp body of the dire wolf leader lay far below, impaled upon the jagged rocks. It seemed to float in its stillness, suspended with its monstrous head and hind quarters drooped at either end of twin spires. He turned away and closed his eyes, the thin membranes sliding from the side over his minuscule bulbs until he saw nothing. His thorax tightened.

Despite the ferocity of these wolves, he didn't think them evil. They were merely apex predators of the natural world.

Still, we had to drive them from the vale, back to the forest.

This was a victory. Even so, Siv didn't feel good, and he

didn't understand why. The plan had played out beyond his hopes. Young Atul had been brilliant as his stag.

And yet... only emptiness.

He lowered himself to the ground, troubled. As council seer, he had always guided the vilskje with clarity and ease. But the red tide had changed everything. The omen had shaken his confidence and instilled doubt until he found himself second-guessing every thought. He didn't know where the dire wolves had been hiding for so long in Glimryn Forest. It was puzzling that, before now, not one had entered Windlyn Vale in all these centuries.

Puzzling... or impossible? Could they really have survived the Calamity only to hide unseen in the forest for all this time?

The Great Tome, the vilskje's one source of documented knowledge, described the dire wolves, and there was no doubt that these predators matched the description. The Tome made no mention of the Calamity, however. Surely because it was written before that world-changing event had eradicated nearly all the living creatures of the world, reducing the planet to a barren wasteland known as the Eternal Desert. Only Windlyn Vale had been spared, shielded by the awesome power of the Father of Light.

Siv lifted himself from the ground and took a deep breath, dismissing his thoughts for now. He turned back to Atul and released the blackness of his vision.

"I think it's time we return."

"I'm ready, Seer."

Siv watched as Atul transitioned to his hawk. It was one of the clan's largest, nearly six feet from tip to tip. A rare species that roosted high on the cliffs and soared over the vale, claiming unsuspecting prey on misty days.

Siv shifted to his gannet. It was a modest form in some regards, but blessed with superior instincts of the sea. He signaled Atul over with a wing, and the two walked to the edge to look over the broad expanse of their homeland below.

Atul turned to his mentor and spoke in the throaty voice of the hawk. "Siv, how can we know the dire wolves will leave the vale now?"

"They highly depend on their pack order. Now that we've killed their leader, they will go back from where they came to reorganize."

He turned to the young vilskje, whose hawk eyes were fixated on him, admiring. The boy nodded, accepting his words like prophecy.

They all take it for granted that I have the answers. That I am infallible.

Siv nodded to his mentee. "Now follow."

He spread his wings and pushed off from the mountain's edge, out into the brisk, early evening air. He turned his head to observe Atul in his periphery, following him in his hawk form. The younger vilskje accelerated, catching up to Siv.

"Where did they come from, Siv?"

"Somewhere deep in the forest. It's the only place they could have gone unnoticed. It puzzles me that we've never seen one before. But for all our centuries in Windlyn Vale, some sections of the forest may yet remain unexplored."

The cool breeze combed through Siv's feathers and

filled his lungs. "After all, we have everything we need here in the vale and along the coast."

Siv fell into a steep descent and Atul followed, passing him. Siv's gannet couldn't match the agility of the hawk at these heights, nor could he match Atul's youthful exuberance.

Atul expanded his great ash-colored wings and turned skyward with a blast of wind. "You were right, Siv. Look!" he shrieked with joy, gesturing one wing mid-flight in the direction of the tree line to the west. "They retreat into the forest, just like you said." He dove forward with excitement, falling even faster this time. "Siv, the seer!" he shouted back. "I shouldn't have questioned you."

The child thinks too highly of me.

Atul circled back to fly beside him, matching his speed. Joy sparked in his eyes. Siv could tell he harbored a smile beneath that facade of a beak. "I think Wern's right. The red tide was an omen warning us of these dire wolves. But now, we've taken care of them."

Siv shook his head even as he flew. There was something else that bothered him too—a change he'd noticed but couldn't quite grasp. "I fear there is more than this one threat, Atul. Have you noticed how the mists grow thicker?"

"Now that you say that... yes. They do seem thicker, lately. Only in the past few days. I'm sure it is nothing more than a shift in the weather."

"Since the red tide," squawked Siv. "The mists look to me like they're forming one cohesive shape, almost like a reptile. Each day it grows bigger, more explicit in form. It's disconcerting." Siv looked out over the vale below. There were no mists there now, only the sun casting its warm rays over the grasslands. "Let's forget the mist for now, Atul. We should celebrate this win."

The two birds flew in silence until members of their clan became visible below in the meadow. More emerged from the burrow to the north, dyr-shifting to their chosen animal forms on their way out. A few remained in the natural, insectile form of the vilskje, running through the plains grass on six legs supporting their stick-like bodies.

"The clan is flocking," Atul said. "They've seen the dire wolves retreating."

Siv nodded. "They have reason to celebrate tonight. They can take predator form once again without confrontation."

Atul spun in celebration. "We can eat meat again," he shrieked with excitement, and the vilskje in the meadow below reciprocated his call.

Siv swooped lower, catching a current of sea-borne wind beneath his gannet wings. He could taste the salt of the sea and it invigorated and satisfied him. He surpassed Atul, now, who soared closely behind until they both came to land near the entrance of their home. The burrow, a grand rock structure with a cave-like entrance, was comprised of a series of tunnels, which wound like intestines underground beneath the foothills.

Upon landing, the pair were treated with a chorus of approval. Many animal calls mixed with the exultant cheers of vilskje until sounds of celebration filled the vale. The returning heroes lowered their heads in reverence before making their way through the path of boulders that marked the entrance. They nakken-shifted, trading feathers and beaks for their hairless insectile bodies with beady eyes and lipless mouths. Exhausted from the day's task, the pair walked inside.

A vast cavern expanded inside, lit by a bonfire in a pit at the room's center. Descending paths fanned out from this point. The wider path to the right led to the Council Hall, which housed the Council Chamber and its affairs. Further down this same hall lay the sealed entrance to the Progeny Chamber, from which a new spawn, called a broodling, would join the clan roughly every decade or so. Beyond that were large chambers where the council members, like Siv as official seer, took domicile.

Going left from the entrance, opposite the Council Hall, led to the general quarters, where common vilskje took residence among the countless smaller chambers that wound deep beneath the ground. Because Atul was not an official council member, he was required to quarter among the common members of the clan. However, he was of council blood, so he could enter the Council Hall when guided by another member, such as Siv.

Inside the burrow, the two turned right and paused. Master Wern was in the path beside the blazing hearth at the center of the room. At his side stood Yuryk, chief protector, holding his signature shark-tooth spear. Wern stood upright on four legs, with an arm held out in welcome. He scratched at the underside of his small head with his other hand.

"Siv," Wern said, his tone warm, "outside, the vale rumbles from many vilskje feet. I trust you bring good news?"

"Yes," Atul interjected, excited. "We were able to—"

"Not you," Yuryk said, turning his black eyes to the boy and lowering his spear slightly. "Master Wern was asking the council member, Siv."

Wern gestured to Yuryk for grace, before nodding to Siv expectantly.

"Master Wern," said Siv, lowering his head. "We drove the dire wolves from the vale. Their leader is slain upon the rocks at the summit. The pack has fled to the forest."

Wern brought his eyes down to one side before looking back at Siv.

"Outside," Siv continued, "the clan celebrates. They prepare roast pits and scout for herd prey. Tonight, we will eat meat."

Wern nodded. "Well done, Siv. Go celebrate. This red tide of yours, this... omen. You've done well to see us through it."

Siv nodded. "Thank you, Master, but—"

"The tide has returned blue, yes?" Wern took a step forward, his eyes reflecting the red of the bonfire.

"Well, yes it has, but—"

"And our enemy flees, you say?"

Siv nodded, silent now.

"Then, I will hear no more of this omen. The vilskje thrive under your wisdom and my rule. Now go, celebrate."

"Yes, Master Wern." Siv bowed and turned away, with Atul in tow.

On the way out, he saw despair in Atul's eyes where excitement had been only moments before. He could feel the corners of his own mouth turn down.

"Surely, Master Wern will smile upon you when you

return," I had told him. Yet they heap praise on me, while scolding the boy.

"Well done today, Atul," Siv said, turning to the youth. "I'm going to roast you the most tender of vale deer."

Siv watched as the despair lifted from Atul's eyes and he smiled. "Thanks, Seer. I wish there was more I could do."

Siv placed a claw on Atul's shoulder. "Something tells me this isn't over, friend. Stay ready."

ROAST

Outside the burrow, Siv watched the younger vilskje skin and pile the deer into pits lined with leaves. None were over a century in age. They had located the herd at the edge of the vale. At a dip in the meadow near the coastline, the hunting party had surrounded the deer as grey wolves, trapping and killing all eleven—the largest haul of the season. The scouts, who had witnessed the hunt from above in their avian forms, now recounted the story with excitement. All who listened stretched their insectile bodies joyfully toward the sky.

The elders tended to five large fires several yards apart from one another. The flames cast dancing shadows upon the landscape. They erected bone spits over the flames, held up by wooden stands on either side. They smashed herbs from the forest and meadow upon slates and mixed them with salts from the shoreline. They rubbed the spice mixture over the deer flesh and tied the meat to the spits using pyogi vine.

Siv slowed his breathing, savoring the vibrant smell of roast, carried by a soft wind from the sea. Tonight's feast was a rare exception to the clan's staple of root vegetables and raw fish. They preyed on land animals only on special occasions, in times of celebration.

Siv stood in the cool evening, observing. The vilskje, commonly stoic, were animated this evening, their tiny eyes reflecting tranquility from the blazing fires before them.

He didn't share their sentiment.

They're simple. Like the vale deer they feast upon. Running this way or that, to patches of grass, or away from predators. On what grounds do we claim Windlyn Vale? Why do the vilskje deserve this meal, while the dire wolves— natural predators in their own right—somehow do not?

Siv shook his head. A wave of oppressive thoughts had washed over his mind in recent days, just as the red tide had stained their shores. How could he advise when he needed counsel, himself?

Several yards away, Atul transformed to a hawk in the firelight, replaying his earlier heroics to the applause of the surrounding youths. He circled overhead, toppling the invisible wolf over the edge. Elders formed an outside ring and watched, smiling with approval. Delagria and Zurt, two kind and inseparable elders of common creation, stepped inside to cheer with the others. Siv lowered his body a few inches, dissatisfied.

He's a kind soul, but Atul craves the praise of his peers. Unable to see the bigger picture, he doesn't care to peel back the layers.

Siv averted his eyes, looking down at the grass. He had

thought maybe with time, Atul could change, could grow into something greater. But he could no easier change Atul's nature than he could the course of a river.

I love the boy, but he doesn't have the makings of a seer.

By another of the fires, the stalwart Strigo made a show of his giant stag beetle, nearly the size of a dire wolf. A warrior of common creation, he was the greatest of all the vilskje in size, and some would say spirit. His beetle's exoskeleton of deep amber shone in the firelight. It was a form for celebration only, as the vilskje sought to mimic the natural size of the animals they portrayed and, in actual practice, he favored a massive brown bear. Strigo made a show of slashing at the space around him with his pincers as if battling the pack of dire wolves. The warriors of the clan surrounded him, cheering and admiring his dominance.

Siv turned away, toward another of the fires, allowing the aroma of the roast to quell his discontent. A youth appeared and bowed his head, presenting him with swaths of meat upon layered leaf. Siv accepted the meat and took a bite, allowing the membranes to slide over his eyes, bringing blackness to his vision so that he could focus on the pleasure of taste alone. For that one moment, his worries melted away as the tender meat dissolved in his mouth.

Siv released his vision. In the distance, he could see one of the clan standing off to the side, observing the others. It was something he often did himself. He squinted, straining his eyes, until he confirmed who it was.

Ilyana...

The girl was of common creation and a quarter century in years, of similar age to Atul. Ilyana had spoken with Siv early on, since maturing from a broodling. She had never shied away from him on account of his council blood or title, as others did.

Ilyana noticed his gaze and turned toward him. A moment later, she walked over, her thorax upright and tiny eyes affixed to his.

The meat-bearing vilskje returned with another offering, and this time Siv took two slabs, holding them upon a plate of rigid leaves. He chewed one as Ilyana approached, swallowing it when she drew close.

"Ilyana. Do you enjoy the feast?" Siv asked as she stood beside him, facing the fires. He held out a slab of deer meat, which she accepted. Her head was bent slightly, and the corners of her mouth drooped at the edges. Upright, she was maybe four feet tall to his five.

She looked up at him. "Something's wrong... isn't it?"

Her small eyes shone like onyx in starlight. Ilyana seemed to have the ability to pierce his mind, straight to the truth, cutting through objections and inhibitions.

"I... don't know," Siv mumbled.

There was a fondness between the two. An unspoken understanding. But he was reluctant to share his worries with the girl. To welcome her into the fractured state of his own mind.

It wasn't her burden. Yet he wanted her thoughts.

Ilyana seemed to look right through him. "Will you walk with me? There have been whisperings in the burrow. I went to find out for myself, and then..." She hesitated. "I heard you speak of—"

"You were listening in on the council?" Siv whispered harshly.

Ilyana turned away as if slapped before slowly bringing

her gaze back to him. "The rumors were concerning. I wanted to know." She reached out and took his claw in hers. "Please... won't you walk with me, Siv?"

He nodded, and the two walked toward the sea.

RED TIDE

Tiny golden petals of Lion's Mane brushed against their feet as they went. Deeper in the sweeping meadow, the evening wind carried the soft whistle of Bloom Haze, familiar and sweet, to the sensors on their antennae nubs.

Siv paused, turning toward his friend. He let out a deep breath. "Your senses are correct, Ilyana. Tell me, the whisperings in the burrow... do they concern an omen?"

Ilyana turned to Siv, nodding. "Among other things. I overheard you say that word... and something about a red tide."

"Did you share this with others?"

"No. I wanted to speak with you first. But since then, you have been always with your successor or at council."

Siv continued onward, and Ilyana held his gaze as they walked. Beneath their feet, the grassy meadow dipped and swayed all the way to the coast, the bright blue green of the Spyrul Sea expanding in their view as they neared its broad face. He had known he would tell this story to Ilyana at some point.

"It was six days ago," he said, "in the early evening, just as the sun began its fall behind the edge of the world. I was out here alone, in the shallows, pecking mackerel from the mud flats with my gannet's beak. The clan had returned to the burrow for the night."

As they walked closer to the coastline, the meadow beneath their feet became riddled with sand. The grass grew sparse, wicked and tangled, coarse from the ocean's salt. A cast of crabs fled as they approached, barely visible in the moonlight as they scuttled to the side, hiding in the tall grass. The hum of insects from the valley diminished behind them and the soft crashing waves ahead grew more present.

Ilyana's eyes had widened to a speck on a thrush's egg. "You crave solitude, like me," she said. "That's why you came here, alone."

Such rare intuition amongst the vilskje...

"I do."

The two at last stood upon the shore. The moon was full, high in the sky behind them. It cast such light as to suggest, rather than night, a new and different type of day approached. He sat down, four legs in the soft sand, and held his claws clasped together behind his head, with elbows out to either side. Ilyana sat beside him.

"The night of the red tide... it was a calm sea like this. A glint of scarlet appeared in the distance. What I thought must be an odd reflection of light on the waves. But it grew, and the orange and yellow hues around it drowned in its dominance, until the far sea was all a crimson like I had never seen. The sight alarmed me so that I sprang up with fish in beak and flew high, circling above to watch the red expand across the waters toward the shore."

Ilyana looked up at him with concern. "What was it, Siv?"

"At the time I didn't know, but my flesh swam at the sight. The entire sea had turned a violent red, like the blood of a fallen giant. I flew back to the burrow with trepidation in my heart."

"And you told Wern and the council?"

Siv shook his head. "Not then. I didn't know what it was, though there was a tingling of familiarity, something from the past. I needed to consult the Great Tome. I didn't sleep that night, instead scouring its pages for wisdom."

Ilyana got to her feet and walked to the water, to where the breaking waves ran up the shore and washed over her claws. "You speak of the Tome often. Don't you know its contents?"

Siv shook his head. "The Tome's content is vast. It's more a reference than a thing to absorb; attempting which would be a most futile task. And my memory fades further each day, child. Aside from that, much of the knowledge contained within is from the time before the Calamity, before all life outside of Windlyn Vale was eradicated, and therefore, is of little relevance to our day-to-day lives. I have read it all at one point or another, but memory serves me only as it shall."

Ilyana kicked the water with one foot. She turned to face Siv. "And you found the red tide in the book?"

"Yes. The Tome described it as a symbol of great cosmic importance. The red tide itself is a natural phenomenon. A rare occurrence of algal blooms, like a flowering beneath the surface. A short-lived, visual event."

Siv stood and walked beside her, allowing the water to lap over his claws. He looked down at the blue frothing and bubbling tide, remembering that day, seeing it turn red in his mind's eye.

His voice grew thin. "According to the Tome, however, the red tide can also be an ill omen. I fear that Windlyn Vale is on the verge of devastation—of a horrible change I cannot prevent." His voice fell to a choking whisper. "I can't see what this change is, but I *feel* it."

Ilyana took one of his claws in hers. "This is not on you alone, Siv. I feel it too."

He met her eyes. He breathed in the salty air and allowed her presence to calm him. "You do?"

She nodded, turning back to the sea. "There are other troubling rumors, Siv, besides the omen. Though I feel it may all be connected. Have you heard anything about the broodlings?"

Siv frowned, shaking his head. "No. What have you heard?"

"There are whisperings that something is wrong with them. When they emerge from the earth, they are not as they should be. They say it's happened more than once now. Some say as many as three times."

Siv thought back. It had been a while since the last spawn had emerged to join the clan, but had it been three full decades?

"It's just a rumor, Seer. I can't confirm." She turned back in the direction of the burrow. "The clan celebrates.

But those dire wolves aren't the end of this omen, are they?"

Siv shook his head. "I've been trying to convince myself that it's over. But everything in me... the intuition from all my centuries as seer, the gravity of the Tome's words... it all suggests some foul thing yet unseen."

There was a shuffling from behind, and Siv turned to see three vilskje standing in the sand.

"There you are!" said one.

Another jumped in front. "Seer, Wern needs you back at the burrow. Something has happened."

Siv and Ilyana exchanged a concerned glance, and then he took off toward the burrow.

RAYLA

When Siv arrived back at the fire pits, many of the vilskje had retired for the night, but the aroma of roasted meat still hung in the air. Atul ran to the edge of the clearing to greet him. The scouts scurried past them to the burrow, their task completed.

"Seer, I've been looking for you. Where did you..." The boy paused, his eyes falling on Ilyana as she came from behind Siv to stand beside the seer. A slight frown settled on his face and his head dropped a little, barely noticeable in the moonlight.

"What's going on?" Siv asked.

"A girl's gone missing." Atul said, regaining his composure. He glanced backward. "I told Wern I'd summon you. Not many know of this."

"How long has she been gone?"

"Only since the roast, I believe," Atul said. "I'm not sure why the Council is so concerned. I think they are on edge because of the recent attack." He looked away, staring off into the distance. "They didn't share their reasoning with me, though. Just ordered me to find you."

Siv frowned. *This seems like an over-reaction, as the boy suggests.*

"Thanks Atul. I will go see him now," Siv said.

With that, he ran to the burrow. A feeling of dread hung about him like a shadow. Anxiety spread, a thick fog in his mind. As he entered the burrow, he held in his head an image of the crimson tide, clear and vivid.

Yuryk, chief protector and first in command, met him just inside, his face cast dark, shadowed by the fire blazing behind. He turned and walked toward the Council Hall alongside the seer. "Rayla didn't show for the ceremonies tonight. Her progenitor, Kassa, says the girl would never miss a feast."

"Did Wern send scouts to retrieve her?" Siv frowned.

"The scouts searched north all the way to Tevryk Falls and back down along the coastline. They didn't find the child on Mount Svernos, nor in the surrounding meadow. She wasn't at the foothills, nor the cove."

Siv raked his claw along his spindly neck.

That leaves the forest.

They entered the Council Chamber, distinct from the rest of the burrow in its ornate composition of white stone and marble. Yuryk gestured to Master Wern, who sat in his engravement place in the floor, the hollow carved into his near exact shape. The statue of the Father of Light stood above all at the center of the room.

Wern stood as they entered, addressing Siv from across the room. "I'm sure the chief protector informed you that a girl by the name of Rayla didn't attend the feast tonight." His deep voice echoed in the otherwise empty hall.

"Yes, Master," Siv said. "But, with all respect, I'm not sure I understand why the Council is so alarmed. She hasn't been missing long. Perhaps she ate just before, unaware of the upcoming roast."

The master shook his head. "Vilskje never miss a feast. The only place the scouts haven't checked is the forest, where those beasts fled mere hours ago. I'm concerned that Rayla may be in danger."

Siv frowned. "We watched the dire wolves flee after we slew their leader. She was not with them. And I doubt she'd go into the forest of her own accord. The scouts may have missed her elsewhere. She could be trying a new dyr-form, young as she is. She may have had a mishap, light forbid, turning to a rabbit near a fox, hidden in the bush. Or perhaps she shifted to a bass in the Zaqar River only to have a current deliver her into the jaws of a bull shark. I have known them to swim up brackish and freshwater to the point of our foothills."

"All possibilities," Wern agreed. "But I want you to ensure that she isn't another victim to those dire wolves. If she is, recover her body and bring it back here, so she can go through Renewal. Kassa deserves that comfort for her loved one. I may need to order that no vilskje can enter the forest until further notice. It may need to be a permanent measure if we can't be assured of its safety."

The seer stepped forward, the muscles in his mandible tightening.

Wern hasn't always been this irrational. He's certainly on edge recently.

"Permanent measure? The forest is part of our land. You can't forbid the clan from entering—"

Yuryk swung his spear sidelong at Siv, stopping before making contact but blocking his advance on the master. "Watch yourself, Seer. Do you undermine the master in front of the Father of Light?"

Siv stepped back, heart pounding, surprised by the aggression. He brought one claw to his neck, knowing he hadn't been struck and yet still somehow expecting to feel the warmth of his own blood. Wern and the Council were stern, yes, but they had never threatened violence toward him, a fellow member.

Yuryk wouldn't act this way on a whim... it may as well be Wern's spear at my throat. If I hadn't stopped... would he have killed me?

He locked eyes with Yuryk, but the chief protector was the face of stoicism. Siv's gaze fell. He thought of the red tide and the marble floor turned a dark crimson, an angry current rippling the surface. He cradled his head in his claws, clenching down, shutting his eyes. Then, cognizant of his weak display, he dropped his arms back to his sides and opened his eyes.

He took a deep breath, brought his attention back to Wern. "My counsel is to keep the scouts in rotation until we find the girl, in case the situation is as I described. I will investigate the forest tonight, and if the girl is there, I will bring her back."

Wern sat back in his recessed spot on the floor, which cradled his stick figure in smooth marble and cobalt moss. "Very well, Seer. One more thing—you must go alone."

Goosebumps spread over his flesh. Why would they put him in danger, going into the forest at night, alone?

"Surely, Atul can come at least," said Siv. "Or Strigo. His brown bear would be of great help should I run into trouble."

"No," said Wern. "I want this kept quiet. Tell no one else. Did you see all the content faces at the roast, tonight? We won't spread a fresh panic among the clan just after we eased their collective nerves. Only the scouts and a few select others know of the missing girl. All were ordered to keep this to themselves. Strigo, for example, does not know. Atul has done well today, but he is still earning our trust. You must bring the girl back, Seer, and you must do so alone."

"Yes, Master Wern," Siv said, after a moment's hesitation. It was hard to mask the frustration in his voice. "I will do my best."

Atul the Selfless

Atul stood under the soft glow of the moon amongst the smoldering roast pits. He was full from roasted deer, having washed down a third serving a moment ago. Now he lapped up the cool, rushing waters of the Zaqar River with his long, cupped tongue.

He had considered following Siv to consult with Wern, but he was still sore from how the council had treated him earlier. Yuryk had silenced him in front of the master and the seer, despite his brave actions on the mountain.

I save the clan from the dire wolves, and they treat me like this?

Until they showed him respect, he would be in no hurry to consult with them. Besides, the girl Rayla was probably just off somewhere alone. It had only been a couple of hours.

Hardly a crisis if you ask me. Which, of course, they didn't.

Most of the clan had retired for the night, marching like ants to their chambers in the burrow. Atul, however, could not sleep. Too many questions plagued his mind. He finished drinking and walked back to the fire pits.

Why does Siv spend his time with Ilyana? I risked my life for his plan. Shouldn't he celebrate with me?

It was unspoken, but Atul was to succeed Siv as seer. To serve the vilskje in this capacity was something he wanted more than anything. It would be a long time from now, perhaps half a millennium, but he was next in line, as the sole, young progenate of Council origin.

And yet, the Council remains unimpressed with me, even after today. How can I guide them if they won't respect me?

He had thought it was his age, but he wasn't so sure anymore. And a frightful realization was settling in, making his thorax twist and cramp. The tear sacs at the edges of his eyes began to fill.

Siv doesn't truly respect me, either. Does he? He doesn't really talk to me. Never has. He only commands.

Atul paced back and forth by the fire pit, stepping closer and closer until the hot ash burned his clawed feet.

Yet he talks freely with Ilyana, a girl of common creation.

He stood in place even as the earth burned him. He clamped his mandible hard. The tear sacs at the corners of his eyes burst, shooting clear liquid anguish in the thinnest of streams. Steam rose where the tears struck the parched earth.

He thinks I'm not good enough. They all do. Even after today.

No matter what I do, I'm not enough.

Atul stood in place until the pain became unbearable, and then he limped, grimacing, back to the river, where he cooled his feet in its churning waters. The soft current washed his pain to the sea. He closed his eyes and breathed deeply for several seconds, allowing the sound of the rushing river to cleanse his disparaging thoughts.

You're being a fool, Atul. An insecure fool. The Father of Light has presented you with another test on your path to seer.

Convinced of his self-sabotage, he turned back, feeling refreshed, rejuvenated by the river's blessings.

Today, in a selfless act, I saved our clan.

He walked back to the burrow with fresh vigor.

Atul the Selfless. I like that.

He arrived at the entrance just as Siv walked out, looking as dejected as Atul had felt only moments before.

The Cliffs of Glimryn Forest

The council sends me into the forest alone at night, on a whim. Lunacy.

The vilskje didn't venture far into the forest, usually keeping to the edge where they gathered herbs—and only in daylight. Under that canopy, Siv always had the urge to turn back to the open meadows of the vale. The feeling seemed to grow stronger the deeper he went.

Father of Light. I always need your resolve to enter the forest. This night more than ever. But coming back to the glory of the morning sun, shining high over Mount Svernos, will be confirmation of your loving embrace.

He didn't know why they feared the woods so close to the burrow. It must be a survival instinct—that feeling every natural creature of the world had, directing them where to go and what to avoid. He'd like to think, as seer, his sense was superior to most. There was some reason for fear. On rare occasion, the grey wolves would attack a vilskje out wandering alone. Like he was tonight. The dire wolves, of course, were far more dangerous.

I pray they didn't get poor Rayla.

He didn't know the girl well, but she was one of the clan. That was all that mattered.

Siv paused, raking one claw lightly down the side of his face. This whole turn of events made little sense. He didn't know why Rayla would venture into the forest. And it didn't seem right that the Council insisted he go alone. Did they trust Atul so little that he couldn't accompany him in the forest?

He shook his head and started walking, cutting west toward the forest. There was no point in using logic. It didn't change what he had to do.

Something in the near distance caught the corner of his left eye as he turned. A pair of tiny, glowing eyes. The figure approached, and as it drew near, he recognized them as belonging to Atul. Their sparkle suggested good spirits.

"Atul, I'm surprised you're still out here. You must be tired after today's heroics."

The boy smiled. "Your plan worked, Siv. Someday, I hope to guide the clan as well as you."

Siv looked down at the dirt, black in the night aside from the dull flickering of the nearest dying fire. At times like this, it was difficult to deal with Atul's superfluous optimism.

"Thank you for the kind words. But a foul air still hangs about. Can't you smell it?"

Atul looked to one side, his antennae nubs twitching. Then he looked back at Siv with the same bright eyes. "I only smell the lingering aroma from our celebration. But if trouble comes, I'm always here, Siv."

"By the light—you are a benevolent soul, Atul. I think you should get some rest now."

The boy nodded. "But where are you going?"

Siv sighed. He didn't want to say, but to dismiss him would be rude.

"The Council has ordered me to look for Rayla in the forest tonight."

Atul nodded. "Then I will go with you."

"The Council has ordered me to go alone. I'm sorry, Atul."

The boy paused, and for a second, his eyes appeared to dim. He cupped one elbow with his claws and scraped at the skin.

"Are you sure I can't come? I want to help."

Siv nodded, frowning. "I'm sorry."

Atul shrugged awkwardly. "Okay. I think I may be tired, after all." His voice was soft, a whisper. "It's just hitting me now."

Siv squeezed Atul's shoulder firmly with one claw before turning and walking back in the direction of the forest.

Along the way, he considered how to approach the task.

Fly overhead? No. My gannet may miss the girl beneath the canopy.

Sneak from tree to tree as a fox?

He cocked his head to one side, considering.

Scurry along the brush in shrew form? No, too vulnerable and poor line of vision. I think the fo—

"Siv?" Atul's voice rang out from behind.

Surprised, Siv turned back. Atul's silhouette was facing him, black, a shadow figure, the light of the burrow's entrance at his back. "No one else is helping you tonight, right?"

Siv paused, trying to decipher the reasoning for the question. He shook his head. "No. I told you. I go alone."

He could make out a shadow of a nod before the boy disappeared inside the burrow.

That was odd.

With a shrug, Siv turned back to the forest, where the trees stood the height of a mountain.

Siv stood in the forest, facing darkness. The moonlight from the vale had slipped further behind him with each step. He rubbed his fox paw against his whiskers, brushing off dirt that was not there. He had a growing urge to abandon the task, to break for the tree line. He could be in his grass bed back at the burrow in less than half an hour.

But what if the Council's right? Could Rayla be lost in here, or worse, have fallen prey to the dire wolves?

He needed to know.

So, he pressed on. He soon came to a familiar clearing where the trees were scattered and bushes grew in thickets. Here, plentiful herbs and wild berries grew, and the vilskje would come to pick and gather during the day. Moonlight penetrated the loosened canopy overhead, granting Siv the courage to continue. He crept along the ground, scattering fallen quia nuts and inhaling the aroma from the herbs so often used in vilskje roasts. He chose a path that hid his burnt orange fox fur with complementing flowers and leaves. His furry ears were erect, listening for any sounds of the dire wolves or of the girl. He heard nothing, so crawled deeper into the forest.

Beyond the clearing, darkness returned, to where he could see only a couple of feet in front of his nose. His stomach tightened into a knot. It was silent, aside from a few night birds high above the canopy, which seemed more and more as if they were in another world. He turned back, half-expecting to see Atul behind him and almost wishing for the boy's company in this place.

There's no sign of the girl. There doesn't even seem to be any animals this deep in the forest.

A toadstool emerged between two trees as he moved through the forest, then three of the mushrooms, then five, until at last he came to a second clearing. The moonlight shone more dimly here, this deep into the forest where the trees dispersed only so much. And yet, it seemed bright as a morning in the vale compared to the stark blackness from which he had just emerged. The clearing was cobbled with giant mushrooms. White, emerald, and hazel, the edges of their toadstool caps touched, creating a fungal mattress the height of his snout. They crowded together as if star gazing through the opening in the canopy above. Golden speckled butterflies fluttered about. Siv paused and stared at the clearing with wonder. There had been no accounts of this place that he could remember.

How is it that no vilskje has ventured this far into the forest before?

Siv's fox tested the fungal mattress with a paw before prancing atop and wandering forth, slack-jawed and gazing about. At the center of the clearing, his stomach inexplicably tightened, and he doubled up with pain, holding his gut with one paw. He turned back then, and relief spilled over him as he faced the direction of the burrow. He took a step forward and the tightening in his stomach relaxed. His heart leapt into his throat at a sudden realization.

The forest itself is doing this to me. It wants me to turn back.

But why? And how is it doing this?

He felt a thousand eyes upon him, then. The eyes of the forest. He found a nearby gap in the toadstools and squeezed beneath to the forest floor. He hugged the ground, listening. There was no sound of the wolves. Nor of Rayla. There was nothing at all.

Surely, I would have heard her by now.

This is far enough.

Yet he stayed his paw. For a second, he didn't know why. Then he realized.

The edge of the world…

He had already come this far. He needed to see it for himself.

Long ago, the Calamity had destroyed nearly all the living things of the world, reducing the planet to a barren wasteland referred to as the Eternal Desert. There was no written record or explanation, yet the clan had passed the lore down from generation to generation. Only the region of Windlyn Vale had survived, untouched, shielded by the divine protection of the Father of Light—the Watcher. He had saved the vilskje. Now they honored him with a statue of his likeness in the Council Hall. Siv sought the Watcher's guidance often, and he knew his love.

Siv paused now, closing his eyes.

Watcher, guide me…

A warmth spread through his furred breast and over his shoulders, all the way to the tip of his tail. He opened his eyes with new clarity. Windlyn Vale, the last remaining bastion of the world, was bordered by the sea to the east, and falls to the north. But it was the cliffs beyond this forest which marked the perimeter to the south and west. He had seen them in the distance, atop the canopy, but he had never ventured that far, neither above nor below. To his knowledge, no vilskje had ever gone to them.

Tonight, I will go there.

Siv stood and turned around. Immediately, the tightness returned to his stomach. He crawled beneath the mushrooms until he reached the edge of the clearing and plowed forward through sheer will into the deepest stretch of the forest.

Each step was a misery worse than the last. If he was wrong about his solitude, if one of the dire wolves were indeed close by and caught him here, he would be easy prey in his current state. This stretch of the forest seemed to go on forever, and Siv retreated into his own head, trying to will the vice-like cramps away with his mind. At last, just as he'd reached his limit and needed to turn back, he was there. Light broke through the trees less than five feet ahead. His mouth fell open and he willed himself forward and out of the forest. The light of the moon illuminated the cliffs, which rose to the sky like a towering giant. Somehow, an even deeper silence hung about this place. No birds flew overhead. No insects crawled below. The trees closest to the cliff grew away from it, rising at an angle as if to flee.

It was a sentiment Siv shared.

He had reached the edge of the world. It was time to go back.

His gaze fell to the ground in this place where no acorn or leaf dared rest, and his vision blurred. The bare soil beneath his feet turned the deep crimson of the red tide, and he cupped the sides of his fox head with two paws, fighting off a wave of nausea. Weakness overcame him, driving him to nakken-shift. Everything inside screamed for him to turn away from this wall, to flee back to the vale.

I must leave this place before it kills me.

But before he could turn away, a searing pain pierced his gut with the pointed focus of a boar's tusk. Siv groaned, gasping, struggling to breathe as he fell forward. He reached out with one arm to catch himself with the cliff side. But, to his surprise, the wall gave way, bending back like a web beneath his weight, and he collapsed into it. Siv shouted out in surprise, reaching with his other arm to steady himself, his heart pounding.

The wall felt sticky on his palms. Not the thick kind, like tree sap, but more like prey blood an hour after the hunt, when it was still drying. As the wall bent, it held its perfect stone illusion, until the tip of one of his claws tore a small hole through it. Blinding light streamed through the hole, forcing Siv's eyes closed. He gasped in surprise. He pushed a claw from his other hand into the hole, stretching it. Then, with all his strength, he wrenched outward, tearing the sticky substance wide apart. Eyes shut, he could feel the wall rip beneath his claws until he imagined it was large enough to fit his entire body through. At that point, it shook and sputtered in his hands. There was a sound like a whale breaching on the sea, and then he felt nothing at all.

Siv cracked the vertical membranes covering his eyes, waiting for his vision to adjust to the overwhelming bright light before opening them fully.

He gasped.

The entire cliff wall was gone, leaving no evidence it had ever been. Siv reached down and rubbed his thorax where it had been throbbing only moments before. There was no pain now. It had disappeared along with the illusion cliffs.

Beyond where the cliffs had been, a gentle slope descended to a narrow river. A small path on the other side led over rolling hills and thickets. Trees lined the horizon—another forest where one should not have been. Dark clouds appeared in the distance.

Siv stood, dumbfounded, for what seemed an eternity. He closed his eyes, and opened them again, realization hitting him with the force of a cascading boulder. He lowered himself to the ground, curling his claws so they dug into his palms.

Watcher, how can this be? This is no Eternal Desert...
The Calamity... is a lie?

Tempest

Siv dyr-shifted to his fox. He felt vulnerable in the open space beyond where the cliffs had stood only moments before. In the moonlight, he could see with his fox's keen eyesight small fish darting this way or that in the narrow river, its clear waters running south just beyond the forest's edge at the bottom of a gradual slope. Impressions in the mud ran up the bank on the other side, a trail leading from the river to the short grasses where they disappeared in the rolling hills.

As he walked beyond the cliffs, he found it hard to draw breath, so shocked was he at what he was seeing. This should have been a barren wasteland of sand and dusty winds, not this lush place—even in the night as inviting and full of life as Windlyn Vale.

The implications sent his mind reeling to a dark place. If the Calamity was a farce, then who was the Father of Light? It would have been easy to dismiss it all as lies, but he had felt the Watcher's guidance. He had known his love in the deepest center of himself. Their deity was real. But if he hadn't saved them from the Calamity, who *was* he?

Weak and confused, Siv stumbled down the bank until he came upon similar markings in the mud on his side of the river. They looked fresh. He walked over and inspected them closely, his snout in the mud. The scent was like the Zaqar river, making this new place seem even more like an extension of Windlyn Vale. He inferred the markings looked bipedal in their spacing, and their shape was clearly not vilskje. Siv paused on his hindquarters, bushy tail darting around.

He thought of the statue of the Father of Light in the Council Chamber. Their deity's likeness was that of a human man. He'd known that for some time, having matched it to an illustration from the Great Tome.

These markings almost look like those from a human foot.

They formed a trail toward the forest, stopping at the precise location of where the cliffs had been. From that point, they retreated to the river, only to turn back and test the cliffs again a little further south.

Whatever it was... it had been exploring. The same illusion had stopped it from entering Windlyn Vale from the other side.

A sinking feeling set in. He thought of the omen.

I just destroyed a barrier to our home....

If whatever made these prints comes back, there will be nothing to stop it now.

A sudden gale from across the river nearly sent him sprawling to the forest. He looked to the west, surprised by the strength of the wind. Black clouds gathered over the trees in the distance. They spread through the sky like impending doom. The storm had appeared out of nowhere.

Did I somehow create this by destroying the barrier?

A fierce blast of wind pushed Siv to the edge of the forest.

I must warn the others.

He crouched and launched upward, his fox finding surprising height, and, at the apex, he shifted to his gannet, trading fur for feather, snout for beak, and claws for talons. He flapped his wings furiously, rising with the face of the forest, eyes to the sky. At last, he came to land atop the canopy.

Siv turned to face the approaching storm, jerking back with surprise. It was closer than he had expected, its dark fingers reaching now over the river, mere yards away. Rain fell in the near distance and lightning streaked downward in jagged paths, followed closely by thunderous booms. Ferocious wind pushed him across the canopy toward the vale and he spun to the air, flapping to gain control and eventually finding it facing away from the storm. He soared over the forest, suddenly and intensely thankful for all the time and practice he had in this avian form.

Siv arrived at the vale soon after, the landscape opening below as he reached the edge of the canopy. He could see the entire region from here—Mount Svernos ahead, Tevryk Falls to the north. The forest swung around to the south in a hook, bordering the region where the Zaqar River ran east to Holidae Cove before emptying to the Spyrul Sea.

This is only one piece of a larger world...

Beyond the edge of the forest, Siv dove straight for the burrow. He would be lucky to make it to shelter before the storm was upon him. Halfway down, a crack of thunder came from behind, and where there should have been wind protection from the forest, a sudden gale sent him sprawling. He flipped, disoriented, flapping toward the ground then correcting to the sky with all his might, straining his body. When he finally regained control, he had soared well beyond the burrow, pushed by the tempest's invisible hands.

Another gale, even stronger than the first, took him with determined force all the way to Mount Svernos. He slowed enough to avoid a dire crash upon the mountainside, where the wind held him to the stone like the stubborn hand of a giant. Persistent in its toying—not wanting to squash him, but to hold him there for its twisted amusement.

Finally, the wind relented enough for Siv to peel his head from the sheer cliff. He was perched on a rocky outcrop jutting from the side of the mountain. Several feet below lay the common pass.

If the wind holds for just a few seconds, I could slide down to the pass and—

Lightning crashed down, followed by deafening thunder. Black clouds hovered overhead and pelted the mountain with heavy rain. For the second time, Siv wondered if he had somehow spawned this tempest by breaking the barrier.

Any idea of braving the storm abandoned, Siv looked for shelter. There were no caves on the route below, nothing beyond sparse trees and bushes that would be useless in this relentless tempest. Frantically, he scanned his surroundings, finding only the sheer cliff. But off to one side and above, he found something. A giant pyogi tree grew from the mountainside, its root ball partially exposed.

There's a gap. I might squeeze beneath those roots until this passes.

Another bolt of lightning sent him scrambling up the sheer cliff. He pulled himself up the lip of the small ledge just beneath the tree and scrambled to the back of the small, protected area. Drenched and exhausted, he turned to face the storm. He was desperate to sort out his thoughts on the day's events, to form some semblance of understanding. Instead, he closed his eyes, buried his head into his feathered chest and eased backward to rest his tail feathers against the mountain side.

Curiously, he felt nothing there.

He turned slowly around, opening his eyes, water dripping all around, soaking the ledge. To his surprise, there was a small open space in the mountain beneath the root ball, about two feet tall and wide. Siv took a step closer, straining his eyes.

Is this a tunnel?

It would be easy to miss even in the day. From below, it would appear as a shadow beneath the tree. From above, it would not be seen at all. He shook off his feathers, stretched and retracted his wings, and bent low, stepping into the dark space.

A second later, his beak touched rocky soil.

No. It's only a hollow.

An even louder crack of thunder made him jump, and he knocked his head on the stone ceiling of the tight space. He spun to face the storm, seeing a waterfall of rain at the entrance.

At least I can rest here until this—

Another flash-bang cut Siv's thoughts off as lightning crashed upon the mountainside. A rumbling and creaking followed, so close as to seem in his own head.

Is that noise from the tree above?

Goosebumps raced across his flesh, and he teetered forward slowly as the creaking continued, growing high pitched. Rocks fell from the crude ceiling, one onto his back, several more in his path. A deep groan from above confirmed his suspicions.

In a panic, he shot forward and launched himself into the storm, closing his eyes.

Watcher, help me.

He circled back and opened his eyes just in time to see the tree, now split nearly in half, collapse, covering the hollow. His heart beat furiously.

I was nearly trapped.

Siv turned his head toward the burrow. He could see the back of the storm, a sliver of soft blue near Glimryn forest, a respite beyond this violence.

If I can just suffer this a bit longer, I can make it.

Siv banked in the burrow's direction, flapping with all his might. But once again, a purposeful gale took control, spinning him eastward. Near the coastline, a crosswind like a poison arrow forced him north and then down into Gald-hopiggen Swamp, the region between Tevryk Falls and the sea.

Siv tried to abort course, to pull up and away from the approaching bog, but a moment later, he was stuck, beak-down in thick mud, choking. He wriggled his head from side to side, forcing enough space for a small breath, which he gulped with desperation. He took another, but the muck ran into his gullet and he choked and spat. He twisted and shook furiously, struggling for breath, drowning.

But just as he resigned himself to this inglorious death, he inexplicably found his lungs full of air. Murky, dank air —but air nonetheless. He coughed and spat, took another breath, and opened his eyes. He was stuck head-down inside a tunnel beneath the swamp.

What the...

A wretched smell filled the air, and still it was a welcome respite from the angry storm that lashed his hindquarters above. He squirmed and wriggled, trying to break through the small opening to fall inside the tunnel, with no luck. Eventually, desperate to break free, he tried to think of a dyr-form that would allow him to slide into the tunnel below. To his dismay, he could think of nothing better than a snake—an animal he despised and one which he had vowed to never take the shape.

Still, this was a desperate time and not one for ideals. So, he closed his eyes and conjured an image of the vale adder, often found sunning among the rocks at Holidae Cove. He thought of the details of its scaled body, its forked tongue, sharp fangs, and slit pupils. Then, he triggered his cells to make that change.

The shift was crude and sloppy, some of the details were off, but a snake he became nonetheless and, once in the form, he easily slipped through and fell in a curled heap to the tunnel below.

Mud piled and water splashed onto his scales until he slithered to one side, out of the way. He looked up at the hole to see the muck congeal and clot like a wound until the dripping ceased.

He stuck out a forked tongue, thinking, in awe at what had just transpired. It reminded him of the Progeny Chamber back at the burrow, where a new member of the clan was born roughly every decade. The broodling would scratch and claw beneath the surface until the ground cracked and a neonate would emerge from the earth. It would topple at the surface, gasping and shaking. The hapless bundle of fleshy twigs would roll to one side as the ground closed beneath it, the birthing scar healing. It would be years before the young vilskje would have the power to shed its nakken form for other appearances.

Just now, I was like a spawn in reverse, digging beneath, struggling to emerge in this place.

He caught a glimpse of his tail and hissed in reprehension at the sight. He shifted to his shrew, shook off the wet fur, and crawled precariously forward through the murky tunnel beneath Galdhopiggen Swamp.

THE BLOOD BUSINESS

Siv crept on padded feet over the cavern floor, sniffing at the air and squinting in the darkness. The stench hung thick beneath the swamp, complex and unfamiliar. The hairs on his body stood erect and his whiskers twitched with discontent at each drip of water.

Something's in here. Maybe more-than-one-something. I can feel it.

And that smell...

The tunnel was spacious in his shrew form, though it couldn't have been more than three feet in height. He followed a bend to the right, the pungent smell growing thicker with each step. More tunnel stretched beyond and he followed its path, enchanted by a curiosity of what lay beyond. Thunder boomed outside. Light streamed in from another bend on the path before him, providing just enough for him to see.

He followed the path around with his shrew nose to the ground and looked up.

He froze.

A pair of giant yellow eyes floated in the space ahead. Glowing, discerning eyes, oval like the quia nuts scattered about the forest.

Siv's tiny heart pounded. What manner of beast would he meet here in the dark?

A snake the girth of this tunnel! Most vile of animal forms. Mutated and ancient, its body winding behind, down the length of this path to its nest. Hidden for all this time, growing bigger, longer. Lonely, angry, deprived of sunlight. Feeding on unsuspecting trespassers like me...

There was nowhere to flee. This was it. The snake would eat him, preserving the secret of this place.

There was a snap, a sudden spark, then a red light cast the tunnel aglow. The creature that stood several feet in front of Siv was decidedly *not* a snake. It held one five-fingered hand up at its side as if clasping delicately the smallest of twigs, but, instead, a controlled flame swirled atop its fingertips, nearly half a foot tall, and half that in width.

It stood at near the height of the space, its body the color of midnight. Long, pointed ears stuck out from the sides of its robust head, the tips grazing the sides of the tunnel. It wore a grey cloth held in place by a single shoulder strap. One end of its mouth was turned down in contemplation.

An image of one of these creatures flashed in Siv's mind. A memory. The thing floated in the air, cross-legged above a stream, surrounded by dazzling lights. It was an illustration he had seen in the Tome. He mouthed the words that came to his fuzzy maw.

Pixie...

He wondered how a pixie had come to be in Windlyn Vale. How it had survived the Calamity and stayed hidden all this time, like the dire wolves. But then he remembered the other events of this day. The vanishing barrier and the lush lands beyond. He remembered how, though nearly a millennium in age, he knew nothing real and true about the world he lived in. He remembered how much of a fool he truly was.

"You... are not a shrew," said the pixie after a long pause, cocking his head to one side, voice calm, even-tempered. "The whiskers are too long and the nose too short. You smell like the earth... like one of *them.*"

Siv took a step back on his padded feet, unsure of what to do. The description from the Tome took a middle ground with the species.

Mischievous, but not quite evil.

Calm, yet dangerous when crossed.

Surprisingly powerful in concentrated groups. Clever magicians.

For all the failings of his memory, passages from the Tome materialized in his head with crystal clarity when they wanted to.

"But how?" asked the pixie, tapping his cheek. One eye narrowed. "How did you go behind the falls?"

Siv somehow found his voice. "Tevryk?"

"Yes. How could you?" His eyes grew wide, and he nodded. "That's it. The spell weakens... after all this time."

At that, the pixie produced from a pouch a dagger of the most wicked variety; the blade curving sharply from base to point. It held the knife opposite the flame and smiled, revealing pointy teeth, small daggers in and of themselves.

"Tell me, vilskje, how long have you had your eyes on this place? Don't lie. I can be fancy with this." The creature took a step forward, twirling the dagger in its nimble fingers.

Siv took a deep breath, rubbing his nose with his front paw in a feint of nonchalance. Then he stuck his head up, defiant, ears flat against his head. "I didn't come here through Tevryk Falls. My clan has no knowledge of this place."

The flame flickered in the pixie's hand, waving with his quivering finger. "If not by the waterfall, then how? There's no other way."

A series of images flashed in Siv's head. The red tide and the dire wolves ascending the mountain. The disappearing cliffs and the storm that had forced him here.

"Do you hear the storm outside?" He pointed one digit up at the ceiling. "Its winds strangled me in their grip and drove me, reeling, deep into the swamp. I was drowning. I thought I would die, then. But instead I fell into this place... if only to die by your blade." A crack of thunder from above supported his account.

The pixie crouched, holding the flame near his face. He inspected Siv, squinting. "So you haven't been sniffing me out? Not once?"

Siv stood on his haunches and held up both paws in a gesture of conciliation. "Honest to the light, I didn't know of this place before tonight."

Several seconds passed, then the pixie frowned. "I think..."

He stood up, put his dagger away, and brought the now empty hand under his bare chin, rubbing thoughtfully.

"I think you're telling the truth. So, I won't slice you up. In exchange, you only need give me your oath."

"Oath?"

"I have two choices. I could kill you or divulge to you my business here. Neither is ideal. But I don't eat false shrew... and you don't seem otherwise worthy of a kill. So, divulge it is."

Siv shook his head. "I'm happy enough just to remain in one piece. I'll leave once the storm passes, like I never was here..."

The pixie's eyes flashed in the dark. He smiled, then shook his head.

"Oh, no. That won't work, vilskje." He sighed as though his words were a great tragedy. "Tonight, curiosity has been planted like a seed in your fertile mind. You might try to ignore it, but it will grow. Faster than you expect, it will consume you. Then you will come back, with others."

Siv shook his head. "I won't come back, I prom—"

"Then I would have far too much slicing to do," the pixie continued, tapping a finger on his stout cheek, ignoring Siv's words. "It would make a mess of this hallway. It would dull my blade. It would be *very noisy*. That will not do."

The pixie stepped forward, crouching again with his flame. "Instead, I will tell you of my operation, and you will protect my profits by keeping your maw or beak or fish lips —or whatever your real mouth is called—shut about it forevermore. A partner in secrecy, if you will."

Siv strummed his whiskers with the sharp tip of one

digit. "How can you be sure I would keep your secret once I leave?"

The pixie stood up, dismissive. "Because you are one of the vilskje. I've read up on your lot. Trustworthy. Entirely without a clue. It's all part of your condition. What better species to keep an oath?"

Siv's face grew hot. "The Great Tome says no such things about my kind."

The pixie gave him a confused look, his eyes flicking left then right before returning to Siv. Suddenly, his mouth opened in joyful revelation, and he gasped. "Of course. Like children!"

The pixie cocked his head to one side, stroking his cheek and staring at Siv with new wonder. "Tell me, now, did you believe your species had the only book of knowledge in the world?" The pixie's mouth and eyes clamped shut, expectantly, as if Siv's next words would be the most delicious morsel worthy of his undivided attention.

Siv's silence told the pixie everything he needed to know.

His eyes shot open and rolled back in his head. He shook with laughter.

Siv's blood boiled. A rare, violent impulse had him consider changing to his fox and leaping at the pixie's throat. But the creature's neck was tucked away beneath his robust head, and Siv had better self-control than that. He took a deep breath and held it in, forcing his anger to subside.

The pixie regained composure, placing a hand over his mouth and clearing his throat. "Forgive me. I shouldn't have been so callous. We've gotten a little off topic. The point is this: I trust you will keep your end of the bargain. So, do you accept?"

Slowly, Siv nodded.

"Say it."

"I accept your bargain."

The pixie nodded. "Then, it is done. No need for formalities. Now follow me."

He turned and walked, his flame casting bright orange light on the walls. Siv followed, and the pixie turned his head back every so often as he spoke.

"They call me Drexel. I'm a traveling merchant of the Fallbright pixies. Our chorus is far west from here, beyond mountains that make your Svernos look like a step stool. There might be giants if you go that way, so always look up for falling feet. I peddle many things, but what brings me to your little play area of the world... is blood."

Siv stopped. "Blood?"

Drexel looked back, smiling at Siv's discomfort. He winked. "Yes. Blood is my bread and butter." He smiled wickedly, and his eyes shimmered in the dank tunnel.

"But don't worry. I won't harvest yours unless you break your oath. Now wait here for a moment. I need to check on him. I'm worried about your stench. You smell like mud."

"It reeks in here," Siv said. "My scent is subtle by comparison."

Drexel shook his head. "A dragon's sense of smell is refined. A fresh scent can rouse their interest even in deep slumber. Believe me, we do not want to wake Laguznal."

Siv paused, his mouth falling open. He thought of how the mists had grown thick over the vale in the days since the red tide. They would drift and form only to disappear and come back the next day even more defined and purposeful. A massive shape, with great wings. Siv mouthed the word he had thought before but was afraid to speak... *dragon.*

The Tome described dragons as powerful, fire-breathing lizards of legend. Intelligent, territorial beasts. And, according to vilskje lore, extinct since the Calamity.

If the Calamity is fiction... then dragons could still exist. But right here in Windlyn Vale?

Siv opened his mouth to speak, but Drexel had continued on, descending the tunnel ahead and disappearing at yet another bend in the path. The pixie brought his magical light with him, leaving Siv in the dark aside from a glow on the wall ahead, opposite the bend. He stood in stunned silence, the tunnel's pungent smell taking new, deadly meaning, unsure if he should follow.

A few moments later, Drexel returned. "He still sleeps," he whispered. "I'll take you close, but we must be quiet." He beckoned for Siv to follow.

As Siv descended the sloping path, he strained his memory for more details on pixies. Any mention of mental instability, or made-up games beneath swamps. He found nothing.

"You must be thinking that I'm crazy," Drexel whispered. "Or perhaps that I'm playing a silly game with you."

"No," Siv whispered, suddenly wondering if the pixie could read his mind. "Today's been perfectly reasonable."

Drexel laughed softly. "Indeed." He paused, looking at the trespasser a little less maliciously. "You never told me your name."

"Siv."

"Ah. Well, Siv. I think we'll get along just fine, as long as you keep your end of the bargain."

Thunder cracked and shook the tunnel with ferocity.

Siv cocked his head. "Won't *that* wake this dragon of yours?"

Drexel continued down the path, shaking his head. "Storms do not stir the dragons." He stopped and spun to face the shrew, holding the flame by his face. He lowered his voice. "The Book suggests they dream of thunder."

The pixie's eyes took on the look of a disappointed teacher and he held one chastising finger toward Siv. "A point of emphasis... Laguznal is not *mine*. To suggest so is dangerous. Dragons cannot be claimed. You vilskje have your clan and we our chorus, but theirs is an ancient order. A covenant."

Reluctantly, thoughtfully, the pixie curled his finger inward and returned to the path. "Only fresh smells, I fear, could wake the abyssal dragon. That and my poking and jabbing, but the sleeping agent helps with that."

The further down the tunnel they went, the more humid it became. He could feel it in his tiny rodent lungs. They were heading east toward the sea, he thought, beneath the bedrock that sealed off the marsh above. Siv swatted at an itchy ear and a gnat buzzed off into the darkness. It was hard to believe tunnels wove beneath the swamp.

The path ended at a wide ledge overlooking a vast chamber several yards below. At its center, surrounded by stalagmites, slept an immense dragon. Fireflies hovered about, providing the room with a ghostly illumination. The beast's massive chest rose and fell with each breath, accompanied by a soft rumbling, which had been drowned out by the sounds of the storm. The stench was unbearable here, thick and salty, and Siv thought he could almost see the noxious fumes.

"Laguznal," Drexel whispered, pointing. "Pray his slumber never ends."

Siv gasped. The dragon below lay curled like a typhoon upon the stone floor, vast as the sea itself. Spiked scales of cetacean blue covered its body like grand ornaments, shiny and formidable. Decorative lines raced up its hide, weaving in and out like seaweed or kelp reaching from a great depth to the sun. Long, twisted whiskers curled up the sides of its jaw like mutant krill. If not for the breath entering his lungs, Siv may have thought himself in an abyss, the deepest part of the sea.

The space around the reptile looked curious in its emptiness, though Siv wasn't sure why. Then he remembered a description from the Tome:

Dragons keep in their midst the rarest of treasures.

Drexel made a noise and Siv turned his focus to the pixie, who was watching him with a sly smile.

"You look for coin or jewels. Perhaps a decorative chest?" Drexel whispered.

Once again, Siv wondered about the mind-reading capabilities of the pixies. "The Great Tome suggests dragons keep treasure with them. I see that's not true."

"Ah, but it is. The treasure is inside." Drexel's grin widened, revealing his pointy teeth. "Come with me."

The pixie stepped to one side of the ledge, turned backward, and tiptoed carefully sideways, his arms reaching up for the wall as he moved out of view. Siv walked closer, surprised. The lip of the ledge extended to his left beyond this tunnel, to another space in the wall only a few feet away. Small notches in the wall above provided places to grip.

"Come," repeated Drexel. "The clinic's this way."

Siv followed, balancing his shrew over the ledge until he arrived in a room-sized hollow in the wall above the dragon. Drexel stood there, expectantly, now with a mask over his mouth. Behind him was a wheeled cart with a black skirt, presumably hiding his wares. A colorful graphic of the pixie's face adorned each flap of the fabric.

"What's all this?" Siv whispered.

Drexel's eyes shone, spirits noticeably brighter inside his personal cubby hole. He did something between a bow and a curtsy, smiling with delight. "Drexel Pink, merchant of injections, at your service."

"Please don't tell me you're somehow harvesting this dragon's blood."

Drexel nodded. "Indeed. For years, now. You see, Siv, the dragon's blood is immensely valuable. Before I found this one, I was more of a general merchant. But the fluids trade is too lucrative to ignore, these days."

Siv's whiskers twitched with involuntary trepidation. If the pixie was worried he'd jeopardize this operation, he may just dispose of Siv right there. He stared at the pixie for a couple of seconds with anticipation.

But why even allow me this far? Besides, he said he'd let me go...

Drexel watched him, amused, as though digesting his concerns like a fine stew. There was a prideful luster in his eyes.

Maybe he just wants to show off. One final boast before taking me out.

"You ponder your predicament, am I right?"

"Perhaps."

Drexel sighed. "I've already told you, you remain safe for as long as your mouth remains shut. I'm a pixie, not an imp. We don't enjoy needless killing. Word spreads fast. It's terrible for business."

"How do you even get its blood?"

Drexel removed his mask now, setting it on top of the cart. He had clearly been wearing it for show, the face of the injections master. "Here." He pulled a squirming satchel from behind the black curtain. "This is the secret."

"What is it?"

"Scrivid leeches from your Galdhopiggen swamp, right above our heads. Insufferable things. Disgusting, but effective. They suck the dragon's blood and then I squash them. They're not very smart, you see. All they care about is their immediate hunger. Once bloated, their lives are fulfilled. But what is one leech's life anyhow?"

"A leech cannot latch onto a dragon's scales. You must have found a blemish in its armor."

Drexel laughed. "More foolish tales. Dragons have no soft spots. Their scales are fused to their skeleton like an impenetrable fortress."

"So, the leeches are useless."

"Yes... for all but the cleverest of Pixies." Drexel flashed his pointed teeth in a wide grin. "It turns out that Laguznal sleeps with his tongue hanging out. Unfortunate for him, fortuitous for me. I administer the leeches one after another into that soft flesh and their numbing toxins ensure he doesn't wake. They fall off, plump and euphoric, then I take 'em back here and squash 'em!" Drexel slapped a hand over his own mouth, abruptly aware of his excited outburst.

Siv couldn't help but find himself impressed with the pixie. "But doesn't that foul the dragon's blood, being mixed with the guts from the leech?" He realized after the question that he didn't even know what the dragon's blood was used for.

"Finally, a good question. That was a concern for me at first. But the dragon's blood separates naturally from the leech guts. It rises to the surface just as oils naturally separate from water."

"It still sounds dangerous to prod a dragon, leeches' toxins or not."

"Indeed, it is. But what is life without perpetual risk? Boring, that's what." Drexel pulled a needle with a syringe and a glass vial filled with a green fluid from behind the black curtain. "I do, however, take precautions. This is dreg root extract... most powerful of sleeping aids. The specimen is abundant in your marsh."

Siv nodded slowly, familiar with the herb. The vilskje ground it up and used it themselves as a sleep aid during times of injury or illness.

"This extract is highly concentrated—strong enough to keep the dragon to his dreams. I simply gather more herbs at the end of each trip and bring them back to Fallbright for the alchemy. It needs the pixies' touch to bring it up to working dragon order."

"So you come here for the dragon's blood, and then you sell it to your chorus in Fallbright?"

"Oh, no. The pixies want nothing to do with the stuff.

My best clients are the giants, due west of here in the mountains."

Siv thought of the territorial, bumbling behemoths described in the Tome. It was hard to fathom them beyond ancient ink on the page, as actual flesh and blood.

"You see, drinking the dragon's blood increases longevity. It renews. The giants pay handsomely for it. Did you know, they live only thirty-five years on average? Compare that to your own kind. Or mine. No wonder they covet the stuff."

"The blood makes them live longer?"

Drexel nodded. "Every time. The giants have tripled their life expectancy with my product. For all their petty violence and general ruckus, the giants adore me. So much so that you'll find a carved statue of my likeness at Grayvel Summit, should you ever make your way there."

"You're serious about all this... they carved a statue of you in their mountains?"

Drexel crossed his arms and his eyes rolled to one side. "Indeed. Though it's fair to say the giants are better suited to warfare than the arts. Feeble workmanship at best. The thing looks nothing like me. But it's the thought that counts."

"So why don't the pixies want anything to do with the blood?"

"Dragon's blood has wonderful properties when swallowed, but we pixies already live long lives, and we are ready to go when the time comes. The real reason, though, is they've seen what happens when the blood mixes with your own. It's not advisable to inject it into oneself. The result is... not so good."

Drexel paused, locking eyes with Siv before bringing his gaze to the stone floor, frowning. Behind Siv, the dragon's breath rumbled through the chamber.

"Go on. Tell me."

"When you mix the blood with your own, you are taking communion with the dragons. Do you understand? You are seeking to enter their covenant. It cannot end well."

"How do you know?"

"I've seen it! My damned fool of a brother tried. He burned up on the spot, in front of the entire chorus, all blazing fire and black ash."

Siv held one digit up in front of his maw to quiet the pixie so close to Laguznal.

"Can you imagine a Pixie Dragon?" Drexel continued, still fuming. There was the smallest touch of regret in his voice. "Ralgos, you fool!"

Drexel peered at the sleeping dragon behind Siv, its breathing loud and rhythmic. He took a deep breath, calming himself.

"Anyway, his burning was piss-poor advertising, so now I keep my blood business outside of Fallbright."

"Is there any that could take communion with the dragons? Any who wouldn't burn up if injected?"

Drexel's eyes flashed for a second, lighting up like the fireflies which fluttered about.

The ambition in those eyes... Father of Light...has he thought of trying it himself? Even after seeing his own brother burn alive?

Drexel's words came slowly. "I... don't know. The Great Book back in Fallbright mentions ancient dealings with humans and dragons. Perhaps a human could carry the blood."

Humans...

Siv thought again of the mud prints beyond Glimryn Forest, where there should have been nothing left after the Calamity.

What could have made those prints? Could it be...

Siv stood up on his hind legs, nearing the height of Drexel's kneecaps.

"So humans are real, too? They still exist, I mean?"

Drexel looked somber after being reminded of his limitations with the dragon's blood.

"Of course humans exist," he scowled. "They're everywhere. Like the sky. Like the sea. Like insects which crawl up the leg of your table at supper. One cannot miss them. Unless, of course, you are one of the silly vilskje and never leave your little hidden corner of the world."

Drexel turned to his cart, reached behind the black curtain, and pulled out a flask decorated with a copper leaf draped around the cork. Siv could see dark fluid inside. The pixie held it out in one hand, toward Siv.

"Now that I've given you all the secrets of my operation, we are officially business partners. For upholding your oath, I am granting you a minority interest of... say five percent. This means, in the off chance that we meet again, I may hear your thoughts on the directions of this business, as ignorant as those thoughts may be. I will at least listen."

Drexel pointed to the logo on his merchant cart. "You understand the logos will stay with my likeness. I won't be adding a shrew face here or otherwise. And sadly, your profit share will be zero percent."

He took a step closer to Siv. "However, I offer you this consolation prize..." He held the flask in one hand, turning it in his nimble fingers. "A special, one-time bonus. One flask of Laguznal's blood."

Siv's eyes grew wide. His mouth fell open a little.

"But first, do me one favor. I've not had dealings with the vilskje in the past, and I must see what you *really* look like. I take it your true body will fit in this space?"

Siv nodded. He hesitated for a second but then began the change. His fur retreated into his skin, and he felt his ears collapse like small tents on his head, where they were absorbed. His torso and shrew limbs stretched and grew, and two appendages burst from his midsection in a bloodless affair. He exploded upward toward the ceiling until he was at equal height with the pixie. It all happened in a few seconds.

Drexel watched him with genuine wonder. "Fascinating."

Siv stood facing the pixie on all six limbs, parallel to the ground. There wasn't enough room for the natural, upright position he would commonly employ.

Drexel handed him the flask. "As promised. It won't spoil for centuries. But do yourself a favor. Don't mix the blood."

Siv nodded. He imagined his abdomen as slightly bigger and then, holding the flask to his body, he made that change, encapsulating the flask inside a hollow in his flesh, a process referred to as *pocketing*.

"I've got one more question," Siv said. "You said the vilskje live in a hidden corner of the world. How then did you find us? How did you find Laguznal?"

Drexel smiled wickedly, his pointy teeth glowing white. How quickly his appearance could flip from friend to villain and vice versa.

"Oh, I think that's enough questions."

There was a blur of motion and Drexel pulled something from behind his back. There was a sudden, pointed pain in Siv's neck and he reached up to it and pulled his claw back to see a spot of blood. The tunnel began to spin all around him and everything went grey. He felt nauseated.

I've been poisoned...

Drexel's yellow eyes and devilish grin spun like a swirling sandpit, fading as he fell deeper and deeper out of consciousness. In the growing distance, he could hear the pixie's words, "Farewell, Jaerwin's pet. May we never meet again."

Safe Keeping

Siv woke with his head pounding. His eyes felt heavy as the membranes slid open, revealing painfully bright light. He narrowed them, only allowing them to fully reopen after several moments had passed. He was staring up at the familiar stone ceiling of his burrow chamber. As sensation returned, he recognized a gentle itch from his grass-laden nest beneath his body.

His memory returned, along with vivid images that were hard to accept—the forest and its sticky illusion. The storm, the pixie, and the dragon. It all seemed so real in his head, but he had no recollection of returning to the burrow.

It was all just a dream. It must have been.

"Finally, you're awake. You slept through the morning and most of the day."

Siv sat up. Ilyana was lounging in the guest thatching across his chamber. She was nestled as if she had been there for a long while.

"Ilyana. What are you doing here?"

She stood up, stretched, and walked closer, blinking her tiny eyes. "What happened to you last night? I found you, collapsed outside the burrow. Right after that awful storm passed."

So the storm was real… that doesn't mean the rest is.

Maybe debris struck my head, and I dreamt the rest.

"I couldn't find you when the storm struck. The rest of the clan was taking refuge, and I was worried about you, so I waited by the entrance."

Siv frowned, not wanting to hear the rest.

"You just *appeared*, Siv. I swear I was looking right there… and nothing. Then, you were just *there*, crumpled on the ground, unconscious. One guard helped me carry you inside."

Siv glanced off to one side, trying to figure out his own story. "Wern sent me into the forest for Rayla, but she wasn't there. I remember the storm, but… I'm not sure about what happened. I need time to clear my head, because right now I can't tell what's real."

"So, that's why Yuryk was asking for you. He wants you at the Council." Ilyana walked closer and placed one claw on his shoulder. "Well, I'm glad you're here, Siv. I'll leave you, now, to recover."

She left his chamber. Siv took a deep breath and stretched, raising his arms toward the ceiling. His abdomen felt fat, bloated. He looked down at his body, and it didn't look right. Was he swollen from an injury? He thought of his natural shape and then nakken-shifted, and as he came back to his normal size, he remembered the flask of dragon's blood.

He froze, his breath catching in his throat. His heart-beat thumped in his ears.

No... this can't be real.

The flask fell from the hollow in his abdomen and onto the grass of his nest, no longer secured by the flesh covering. A few seconds later, his flesh finished filling in the hollow and he was whole again.

Siv snatched the flask and held it up to his face. He gasped, dropping it onto the nest again before springing up as if to get away from the cursed object.

It's... all real.

And Drexel didn't poison me, he only put me to sleep.

The dreg root extract...

Siv took a deep breath and then snatched the flask of blood again, holding it close, observing. He tilted it one way, watching the thick, dark fluid move inside.

Dragon's blood.

He stared at the flask, shooting nervous glances at the open entrance to his chamber.

What should I do with it?

He pulled a sharp stone from a pile of rubble on the floor and set it on his nest beside the flask, covering it from view from the archway entrance. Then, he walked over to the wall and removed a heavy stone insert with two arms, heaving with effort to set it down on the floor. He pulled the Great Tome from its safe keep, stroking its majestic cover lovingly as he so often did. He brought it to the bed, where he sat and flipped to the pages at the back section, where the print had worn off entirely.

He hesitated. These worn pages held no knowledge

anymore, but it still didn't seem right to damage the sacred book. Eventually, he relented, rationalizing.

The flask will be safe here, and these pages will be of value once more.

Siv took the sharp stone and paused once more, closing his eyes. He opened them and began slicing through the back pages, carving the layers into a hollow. He did it swiftly but with care, to make a clean shape that would hold the flask snug enough so it wouldn't move about when the Tome was closed.

He stopped every so often to line the flask up, before continuing until he was finished with the task. He placed the flask inside, and stared at it for a moment, satisfied with the fit, but still having trouble accepting the implications of the object itself.

He flipped back through the Tome until he found the section he was looking for:

"Dragons are an ancient species, to be avoided at all costs. They have strong bonds to the elements, whether storm or sea, and they are fierce guardians of their territories. Dragons have established lairs in hidden locales throughout the world. Throughout history, they've been oft mistaken to be extinct, for a dragon will be found only when it wants to be."

Siv closed the book with a sigh. Unsure of what to do, he resolved to keep the blood a secret for now. He was the sole purveyor of the Great Tome. The clan entrusted him, as official seer, to impart its wisdom. Very few of the clan bore interest in its contents.

At least the flask will be safe here.

He restored the Tome for safekeeping behind the loose stone. Stretching, Siv turned to leave his chamber, feeling less groggy. He realized his headache had disappeared.

Now, to address the Council.

Unwelcome

On the short walk from his chamber, Siv considered what he would say at council. He would report about Rayla, but what of the false cliffs? Should he tell them of the dragon beneath Gald-hopiggen Swamp?

I must. I can't keep secrets of this magnitude.

Siv walked down the hall, stopping before the entrance to the Council Chamber, suddenly remembering the pixie. He had given Drexel his word to never speak of that place.

Drexel delivered me here safely. To break the oath would be treachery.

I must uphold it.

Siv entered the archway to the Council Chamber. At the back, Wern lounged in his engravement in the floor. At the center of the room stood the statue of the Watcher. The deity was carved of shimmering white stone. A long beard fell upon his naked chest and his arms were outstretched to either side, casting an eternal blessing over the burrow and his chosen species. Siv found it hard to look upon the statue's face, thinking of what appeared to be the false teachings of the Calamity and the Eternal Desert. He thought of what looked like human footprints in the mud, a species that was not supposed to exist in a place that should have been of sand and desolation. For the first time in his life, he was insecure in his faith.

"Ah, here he is," said Wern from the back of the room. "It appears the storm did not steal Siv from us after all. Thank the light."

Siv lowered his body to the ground in reverence, maintaining eye contact with the clan master. "Yes. I took shelter until it passed. Unfortunately, Master Wern, I didn't find the girl. She wasn't in the forest as far as my eyes or ears could tell."

Wern turned his head to one side, glancing at the guard, Yuryk.

Yuryk stood to address Siv from his place on the flat stone. "Rayla returned shortly after your departure, Seer. It turns out your assessment was correct. She was at Holidae Cove as a crab, feasting on the larva that drift over the shallows where the estuary meets the sea. I apologize for my overconfidence in our scouts."

"I'm glad she's safe," said Siv.

"Was there any sign of the dire wolves?"

"Not one howl. Not a pair of yellow eyes in the darkness."

Wern took a step forward, his arms raised in a triumphant gesture akin to the Father of Light. "Excellent. Then this matter is settled. Siv, you seldom disappoint. A worthy advisor."

Siv turned his head to one side, looking down at the

stone floor. "Excuse the question, Master, but what exactly did I accomplish in this task? The girl needed no rescue."

"Don't discredit yourself, Seer. You warned us of an omen that has proven true, and we overcame it with your guidance. You've driven out the beasts. The girl is safe. We have survived a most unholy tempest."

Siv paused for a moment.

"I fear it's not over, Master. There's more."

The master frowned. "Do tell."

"Last night, I went all the way to the cliffs at the end of the forest. The border that protected Windlyn Vale from the Calamity."

"I don't see how that is telling information."

"It's an illusion, Master. My claw penetrated the cliff. It's not formed of stone. It stretches and bends. It sticks and it tears. And on the other side, a vast world extends as far as the eye can see. Not an Eternal Desert, but a lush landscape filled with vegetation and wildlife, just like here.

Wern took a step closer. "What you speak of is impossible."

"I tore a hole through the cliffs. On the other side was a river, and foothills, and another forest in the far distance. There were footprints in the mud. I think they may be human."

Siv couldn't help but look up at the statue again and his eyes fell to one of the Watcher's bare feet, of similar size and shape to the footprints he had seen.

Wern's face turned red and he was silent for several seconds. Finally, he spoke again. "I see now that we have placed far too much on you, Siv. Your mental faculties are in disrepair. You can only chisel the mine for so long before it collapses."

Mental faculties?

Siv's thoughts turned to the Room Below, a repository deep in the burrow reserved for those who commit crimes, or those of unsound mind. None returned from that place.

"I assure you, I'm quite sane, Master. What I saw was real."

"It cannot be," Wern hissed. "There is no life outside of Windlyn Vale. No humans, no forest other than Glimryn." Wern gestured to the statue at the center of the chamber. "We are in the Watcher's presence. Do you discredit his grace? That the Father of Light saved our species from the Calamity?"

Siv shook his head. "I don't discredit the Watcher, but I—"

"No matter," Wern waved a hand. "We hold you harmless for your words, Seer. Your face droops like a wet leaf, and your back sways. You need rest to regain yourself."

Siv stood still, breathing slowly to calm himself.

"Go now to your chamber and take a respite. We will talk again later."

After a moment of hesitation, Siv bowed his head. He glanced at Yuryk and left the chamber.

Outside in the hall, Siv cursed under his breath. Either they didn't believe him, or they were hiding something.

Or maybe I really am going crazy.

Would I even recognize it if I was?

Siv headed down the hall to leave the burrow. He needed to go somewhere outside of this light-forsaken place to think. But on his way out, he heard something and he stopped. There was a faint sound like weeping coming from one side of the hall. Siv pressed his antennae nub to the wall to listen. The weeping turned to tortured cries, and Siv pulled back in shock. When he put his nub back to the wall, there was nothing but silence.

Was that coming from the Progeny Chamber?

It was somewhere on the other side of this hall. The place where new vilskje emerged from the bowels of the earth, clawing their way to the surface. He thought back to his earlier conversation with Ilyana by the sea. *There are whisperings of something wrong with the broodlings,* she had said. *When they emerge from the earth, they are not as they should be.*

Siv shook his head and walked away, exiting the Council Hallway. He was already overwhelmed. His brain had no room for this new wrinkle.

Back at the entrance, a group of vilskje stood before the bonfire, its smoke piping upward through a thin shaft in the stone ceiling, capped atop the burrow to prevent flooding. Atul was among them, and he approached Siv. "The storm last night was bad, Siv. It looks like you were right about the omen."

Despite his faults, Atul was someone Siv could trust. Perhaps Ilyana was right. He shouldn't shoulder this weight alone.

"There's much to discuss, Atul, if you'll have me."

The boy's eyes lit up, reflecting the bonfire. "Of course. I'm always here, Siv."

The two made their way out of the burrow.

"I found something concerning in the forest last night."

"Oh no," said Atul. "The dire wolves are coming back?"

"Not the wolves, Atul. This is bigger than that. I went all the way to the cliffs at the back of the forest, and..." But he found the words difficult to say.

It sounds crazy. I need corroboration, for my own sake, as much as anything.

"Seer?"

"Will you go with me, Atul, back to that place?"

His mouth opened a little. "Of course, but..."

Siv held up a claw. "Then let's go. I will try to explain on the way, but it will be easier for you to see for yourself."

He squinted from the sun as the two distanced themselves from the shadow of the burrow, which stood like a small mountain in the vale, a child of Svernos made into their home. The day's warmth lifted his spirit. Last night, he hadn't known if he would ever feel its rays again.

He turned to Atul, whispering. "We must be careful. We'll split now and go separate ways to fool any spying eyes. You head to the river, and I will move north toward the falls. Once a fair distance, take to the skies and meet me where the foothills reach the forest northwest of here. Take an indirect path."

"Yes, Seer." Atul's eyes gleamed and he ran southward.

Siv went east through the soft grass of the meadow, turning north to round the corner of the burrow, heading toward the falls. Wind rushed over his body, invigorating him as he sped across the open field. He imagined the clan falling in place around him in herd formation. They shifted to deer and then wolves, following the movement of their leader with guile and grace, mimicking his transformations with precision.

It's been too long since we ran together.

He slowed, turning left to gain his bearings. Movement in his peripheral vision pulled his gaze back in the direction he had come. Someone was running toward him at full speed. The pursuer was still far away, having just turned the corner from the burrow. A moment later, the vilskje shifted and took to the sky. Siv stood and waited, not wanting to play a game of chase or reveal his intentions. As the pursuer drew close, Siv recognized the blue mountain thrush.

"Ilyana!" he shouted, surprised at the sudden joy in his voice. The thrush swooped down in front of him, nakken-shifting to land upon six clawed feet.

Ilyana stood upright, panting. "I saw you leave with Atul. Has something happened?"

Siv didn't hesitate. If there was anyone he wanted to share the past day's events with, it was Ilyana. He had just run into Atul first.

"Come with me atop the forest canopy. I'll explain at the tree line. Atul will meet us there."

He turned and took off running. At full speed, he dyr-shifted to his gannet, gliding just above the tips of the tall grass, inhaling deeply of the salty breeze from the sea. Then he flew left, banking up and over the rocks that made up the roof of the burrow—like the surface of a vast mountain boulder. He turned his head to see Ilyana following, her thrush struggling to keep up with his gannet. The rock expanded below him then he was beyond the burrow, above the foothills covered in tangled thorn and bramble weed.

A few seconds later, he was at the forest. He turned upward, feeling a burst of energy. Patterns of tree bark blurred before him as he sped to the sky. A squirrel darted inside the darkness of the forest at his approach and birds scattered, left and right. At last, he reached the top and came to rest upon the canopy, gripping a branch tightly with his webbed feet.

Ilyana perched beside him several moments later, panting heavily. "I've got… to learn… a faster form."

On another day, Siv might have laughed at that. He might have offered an offsetting compliment on the beauty of her thrush. But anxiety held his tongue as he gazed in the direction of the cliffs in the distance, higher even than these giant trees which they stood upon. Why were the cliffs there now? Hadn't they vanished when he tore through them? What if, when they got to them this time, they were solid to the touch?

And for a moment, he thought it may be better if Wern were right. It may be better if this bubble hadn't popped— and he was simply insane. Windlyn Vale could remain intact, a utopia for the vilskje. Safe and isolated. As it had always been.

But in his heart, he knew that wasn't true.

"I see Atul," Ilyana said. "Look."

She pointed one wing to a massive brown hawk several yards south, looking out to the sea from the edge of the canopy. The hawk took notice of them and flew over, landing on an adjacent tree so that the three birds formed a triangle.

"You brought Ilyana," Atul said, sounding deflated.

"I want to help in any way I can," said Ilyana.

Siv nodded. "I value her input, Atul. Now, let's fly to the cliffs so you can both see what troubles me so deeply."

A Burrow Above

"This is hard to accept," Ilyana said as the three birds flew together over the canopy in a ragtag, mismatched flock, with Siv in the lead. "We've lived in Windlyn Vale forever, yet you claim it's only a small piece of a larger world. I trust your words, but..."

"Yes. It sounds impossible. That's why Wern questions my sanity," Siv said. "I need you both as witnesses."

"I believe you, Seer, but I'm not sure how much this will change things." said Atul. "Would I even want to live anywhere else? Our piece of the world is perfect. We should just stay here, anyway."

The treetops passed beneath them in a blur. Squirrels darted under the canopy and birds cleared their path.

There are animals here now... and I don't feel a debilitating desire to turn back.

"Tell me," said Siv. "Have either of you flown this far over Glimryn Forest in all the years of your life?"

There was a pause then Atul spoke. "I haven't. No purpose, I suppose."

Ilyana chimed in. "I've flown this way before, but for some reason, I turned back. It's like I just lost interest."

"Same as I," said Siv. "Last night, I felt a strong desire to turn back from the forest. At first I thought it was fear, but the deeper I went, the stronger it grew, until it physically pained me to continue. I realized... there was some force trying to keep me away. But once I broke the illusion, the discomfort vanished."

"Look ahead!" shouted Atul. "The cliffs show more clearly now in the distance between the clouds."

Up ahead, grey cliffs towered far above the forest canopy.

"Siv, didn't you say the cliffs vanished once you tore through?" Atul said.

Siv took a deep breath, exasperated.

Could this really have been a dream? Or some cruel trick? If this cliff is solid to the touch... no. It cannot be.

"I don't know the answer. I only know what happened. We'll see when we get there."

Siv thought the coloring of the cliffs odd as they drew closer, but he hadn't seen them in the full blaze of the sun atop the canopy last time.

"There's something now," Ilyana said. "A foreboding feeling, like I should turn back, and an unsettling in my thrush's stomach."

"I feel it too," Atul said. "The uneasy feeling I would get if I swam as mackerel too far into the open sea."

"As do I," Siv said. "Though it's a fraction of what I felt last night. It's puzzling."

At last, the three companions reached the towering cliffs. They rested on the treetops at the edge of the forest.

"Strange how the trees angle back toward the vale," Atul said, head cocked to one side. "How could the wind blow them that way with the cliffs offering protection?"

"Something tells me it's not the wind," Ilyana said, looking down at the sloping trunks.

Siv said nothing.

A couple of yards away, a lone branch bridged the gap between the tree line and the cliff. Siv leaned forward, allowing gravity to pull him over the canopy's edge before stretching his gannet's wings. One flap brought him to the branch, where he teetered precariously near the cliff. Here, he could see that the rock was not opaque—he could see through it, if only slightly. He hadn't been able to tell from afar, for all the lines and patterns of the stones appeared natural.

So, the cliffs vanished when I tore through, but they are slowly recovering...

Siv sighed in relief. His sanity was intact.

Yet, the ramifications were immense.

"What is it, Siv?" Atul flapped his giant wings, diving from the canopy. He seemed to realize late that he would be too heavy for the branch, so he flapped in a circle just above.

Siv felt tiny vibrations beneath his own talons. He turned to see Ilyana's thrush walking up behind him. "I can see through it, Siv. You were right."

He nodded. "It vanished when I tore through, but it's coming back."

"We must see the other side," said Atul. He flapped over to the wall and impaled it with two giant talons. He clasped and pulled at the stretchy substance with his beak.

"Wait, Atul!" Siv said. "We may need the protection of this wall."

But by the time Atul turned back, confused, to look at Siv, his hawk had torn a gaping hole in the cliff the size of its body. A moment later, the entire cliff vanished with a shimmer and the hawk plummeted, squawking horrendously. He flapped his wings until he found the open air beyond where the wall had been. He flew high in a triumphant fanning of his wings before swooping back to the others.

"This is... incredible," Atul said. "Unbelievable."

"You shouldn't have taken it upon yourself to do that," Ilyana chirped, thrush eyes narrowing.

"We didn't come this far just to turn back now, did we? Besides, those dire wolves must have already come through this illusion from the other side. It makes sense now."

"You should have let me make that call, Atul," Siv said, jerking his wings with irritation.

The hawk came to land back at the edge of the forest, looking down at his two companions.

Siv faced him. "Still, I think you're right. There's no going back to the way it was before."

He swooped down from the branch to fly over the narrow river on the other side, low enough to see the footprints, still visible in the mud. More prints led away into the distance.

Something was investigating, but it turned back. Why? Perhaps it felt that same debilitating resistance on the other side.

"Look!" squawked Atul. "A fish with red speckles, here

in the shallows. I haven't seen this type in the Zaqar river." He caught one in his beak and swallowed it down.

Ilyana caught up with Siv on her smaller thrush wings. "I want to see what makes these prints."

The two flew on, following the footprints until they disappeared into a path winding between foothills. Another forest stood in the distance.

"Let's fly up for a better vantage point," Siv said.

Beyond the foothills, round structures covered with what looked like deer hide filled a wide clearing. A fire burned in a circle lined with stones at the center of the large space.

Siv leveled off and slowed to a drift. Ilyana caught up and, soon after, Atul. The three watched as creatures moved about their above-ground burrow like ants. The three birds drifted in a slow descent, an odd trio in a V-formation with Siv in the lead.

"What are they?" Atul squawked.

"Humans," chirped Ilyana.

"Ilyana is correct," Siv said. "According to the Tome, humans are dangerous. I think we should split up. Sea birds do not fly with thrush or hawk. We will draw attention."

Ilyana immediately dropped a few feet, lifting her tiny neck up and chirping. "I'm going down as raccoon to spy. My markings will match well with those thick black and grey reeds at the northwestern corner of their burrow.

Atul swooped left. "I'll circle over the southern edge, where they seem to be gathered. Maybe I can figure what they're doing."

They neared the edge of the encampment now, where the path between the foothills transitioned to open dirt. A few trees grew there. Siv settled on a thick branch near the top of one.

"Be careful, both of you," Siv said. "I'll observe from here for a while. Watch for me. When this tree is empty and I take to the sky, that's your signal to leave this place. We'll meet back at the canopy."

Siv watched as one human, maybe eight yards away, gathered sticks from the ground and carried them back inside the encampment. From between two of the dwellings, he could see the blaze of a bonfire.

Atul circled in the near distance to Siv's left. Ilyana had disappeared from view, he assumed hidden in the reeds on the other side. Two humans came from between the dwellings, walking out into the field, toward Siv but paying him no mind. They turned to each other and spoke, making gestures with their hands. Their voices elevated, but Siv couldn't make out the words. He wondered if he would be able to understand them if he could. One human pointed a finger at the other in what looked like an aggressive gesture then walked off back into the burrow. The other walked around the field for a minute, kicking stones. Then he sauntered back into camp, going a different way.

Siv caught a pleasant scent and breathed in deeply. He moved to another of the nearby trees, where the smell was stronger and his view penetrated deeper into the village. From this angle, he could see a crowd gathered by the bonfire. They held platters and objects in their hands with what he assumed must be roasted meat, which they nibbled upon as they talked with one another. Siv's stomach rumbled. He thought back to their own roast the night before.

More humans came into view by the fire. Some wore cloth around their waist and chest, with an opening going down the middle to reveal tan skin. Others wore cloth which hung down from shoulder to ankle, revealing no skin; these also had hair that fell to their shoulders. Most of the others had shorter hair, though some also had longer hair of varying length and color. They sang together and swayed back and forth. Some locked arms and others kicked their feet and moved their bodies in strange ways as they sang. One of the open chested humans with long dark hair drank something from an object he held in his hands, over and over. He tripped and fell into the crowd. Another laughed and wrenched him up by the arm, patting him on the back and pouring more of the drink into his mouth.

There are so many of them. It looks like they're celebrating.

A squawk brought Siv's attention to the tree where he had just been. Atul perched there now. He turned to Siv and stuck out one wing on the southern perimeter of the encampment. "Siv, look!"

A group of the humans gathered at the southern edge. One held a spear and was pointing behind them, over the foothills, in the direction they had just come. Others held objects like carved sticks with metal components. They were thicker on one end, where the men held them, and Siv didn't know what they were. One of the men brought the object near his face and peered down its length in their direction.

"They must have seen the cliffs disappear. The illusion was on this side too, right?"

Of course, how could they not notice the cliffs disappear-

ing? That's why the footprints turned back before. The illusion made them think it was a dead end.

"I think so, yes. Now, they can see the forest, I presume. Since the barrier is gone."

"But look! The illusion is already coming back, but it looks different, somehow."

Siv turned around, his gaze focusing where the cliffs had been before. As Atul said, it looked different, not like cliffs at all.

"We should leave," Siv said. "Ilyana will follow."

Atul nodded and launched from the tree, his weight nearly snapping the branch. Siv followed and a moment later, the two were over the foothills. Soon after, Ilyana joined them.

What had appeared as cliffs over the forest was a confusing mess on this side. Greens and blues blended with grey in a mishmash of shape and color. It wasn't until they got close that Siv understood what he saw. The illusion was highly translucent now, only just beginning to reappear. The greens from the forest filtered through from the other side, causing visual confusion. The image of the illusion, however, was not one of cliffs—it was a hostile marsh. Cypress knees jutted from moss-laden water and ivy hung from trees over pygmy islands covered with thick grass. It looked inhospitable, untraversable. Far less welcoming even than their own Galdhopiggen Swamp.

So, before, they turned back from this swampland, but now they see the truth.

Standing in the mud as this barrier tried to reassert itself, Siv turned to his companions. "We must get back and consult the Council on this. Atul, tear through it once more so that we may get back."

"But Siv, what will they think once this disappears again? Will it draw them to our forest?" Ilyana asked.

"They will come, regardless. These are explorers."

Atul nodded and flew up to the wall, talons out, ripping and tearing. He pulled at the sticky substance with his beak, stretching until once again the wall disappeared with a splash. A minute later, the three stood again on the forest canopy.

"They are many," said Atul. "And beyond the group we saw, more approach from a path beyond the encampment, from the forest in the distance."

"They celebrate making it this far," said Ilyana. "But you're right, Siv. They won't stop here. These humans are exploring. They want to see what's in this part of the world."

"You got all that from behind reeds at the perimeter of the camp?" asked Atul.

Siv looked at Ilyana with curiosity. It was a fair question.

Ilyana took a deep breath, her thrush breast inflating like a blowfish. "No... I snuck closer. Much closer."

"I told you to be careful," Siv squawked.

"I was!" Ilyana insisted, lifting her wings in a shrug. "No one saw me. I'm good at sneaking. There was plenty of tall grass leading up to the camp. They were drinking and talking loudly and loosely about everything. I gathered much of that information in the first few minutes. The humans are fascinating. There's nothing like them in the vale."

Siv sighed. "This is good information." He looked at Atul. "Both of you. Thank you for coming with me."

"They don't seem dangerous to me." said Atul. "They were celebrating, roasting food that made my stomach rumble. Perhaps we have more things in common with them. Maybe we should even welcome them."

"Regardless, we must tell the council what we saw here. That Windlyn Vale is but a small part of a larger world. That the Calamity is a fiction. I see no barren wasteland beyond our borders. Atul, together we must convince them of the truth."

"Yes, Seer."

Ilyana looked away.

"Ilyana... you know I want you there, but the rules state—"

"Yes, I know," Ilyana said flatly. "No one of common creation may enter the council. Let's just get back. My stomach is growling."

JAERWIN

S iv stood with Atul before the Council. Yuryk, chief protector, eyed him with suspicion.

"Siv? I take it you've had a good rest," said Wern. "I wasn't expecting you so soon."

Siv stepped forward, thorax upright, eyes affixed on the master. "No, Master Wern. I couldn't sleep. Atul accompanied me on a task, the results of which we share with the council now."

The corners of Wern's thin, lipless mouth turned down. "What sort of task?"

"We went back to the cliffs at the edge of the forest. This time, we flew over the canopy. My mind doesn't falter, Master... Those cliffs are illusion. Windlyn Vale is part of a larger world."

Wern stood now from his imprint and looked around, his eyes widening to the size of bubbles frothing in a river's current. "What is this? You expect us to believe—"

Atul stepped forward beside his mentor. "Siv speaks the truth. I saw it myself. I tore through the veil and the cliffs vanished. Beyond the illusion was a river, foothills, another forest in the distance, and… and…"

"And *what?*" Wern turned his head to glare at the boy.

"Humans," Siv said, pulling the master's attention back to himself. "An entire burrow of them, above the ground, with more approaching from the distance. Now that the illusion has been exposed, it's only a matter of—"

"You've ruined everything," Wern said, his face turning a stark red, his entire body nearly doing the same. "I should never have sent you after the girl. I placed her safe return over the welfare of our entire clan."

"You *knew* about this?" Siv found his own face turning red.

Wern ignored him. "Though, I supposed it was only a matter of time, seeing as how the dire wolves somehow broke through. None of it matters anymore." His tone cooled, and his face lightened to its normal shade, before paling to a ghostly white.

Siv's blood went from a simmer to a boil. He closed his eyes and clenched his maw. Behind the lids, he saw himself shifting to his boar and impaling Wern with his tusks. Then he saw the leader of the dire wolves slung across the rocky crags of Mount Svernos, its blood spilling to the path below. That dying wolf became Wern, his abdomen split open and his thin neck hanging down like a vine.

"You knew," Siv hissed. "Yet you insinuated I was going mad. Tell me now what you're hiding."

Yuryk leveled his shark-tooth spear at Siv, taking a step forward. "Watch your tongue, Seer. You are at Council."

Wern raised a hand in Yuryk's direction and lowered it

slowly. The guard lowered his spear, compliant, in line with the master.

Wern took another step toward Siv and Atul. He raised his arms to the vaulted ceiling and looked up to one side, as if appealing to the room at large. "Are seers not supposed to be brilliant minds? What a poor example of one you have turned out to be, Siv. Have you never wondered why the vilskje are born from the ground, clawing our way out for our first gasp of air?"

"It's our way," Siv said. "The vilskje are of the land itself. We are of nature, able to appear as any animal."

"There is nothing natural about us, Siv. We *mimic*."

There was a long silence, and Wern brought his eyes to rest upon the seer.

"If only you could remember," Wern continued. "None can... but me. It is a lonely place, Siv."

"Remember what?" Siv pulled his claws tight together until the joints ached.

"Do you not see how the animals of the vale retreat from us? They are afraid, Siv, because they don't understand what we are. Even you don't understand what we are."

Beside Siv, Atul shook. A small, barely noticeable tremor ran across his body. At last he spoke, flabbergasted. "What are we?" His words came out in a harsh whisper. As brave as he had been in physical danger, these revelations were clearly taking their toll on the boy.

Wern pointed to the statue at the center of the room. "The product of a madman."

Siv clenched his maw tight and released. "The Father of Light?" Before he could stop himself, he broke into wild laughter at the ludicrousness, cutting the sharp tension that had been building. At last, he calmed himself.

"The Watcher is a madman? This is blasphemy."

It can't be true. I have felt his love.

Now it was Wern's turn to laugh. "Blasphemy is for others, Siv. We have no spirituality, for we have no spirit." His voice was pain, and he held an expression to match. His gaze dropped to the floor and his voice fell to a whisper. "Don't you understand? We are not real things of this world."

Siv felt at that moment a new understanding of the master, a pity that he had never felt before. He imagined him, alone in his chamber, on sleepless nights, distraught over the identity of his own species. Alone in his knowledge and unwilling to share. A prisoner for centuries, of his own stubbornness.

Until Siv had forced it from him.

Wern lifted his gaze back to the seer. "That statue depicts our creator, Jaerwin. He is no deity. He is a man who discovered a power that his mind couldn't contain. Eventually, he faded from this world in madness. He saw it coming, and in his final hours he had an epiphany that he wasn't dying—he was transcending to a different plane of existence. He was emerging from a sort of existential chrysalis. He claimed his world skin was cracking and peeling until it fell away."

"Now," said Siv, "*you* are the one that has lost his mind."

"This was the real calamity—his physical severance from us. His dislocation."

Wern turned and walked back to his platform, where he

lay down, contemplating. His anger appeared to be replaced with exhaustion, a relief from finally revealing his secret.

"I think it's true," he continued. "That he's somewhere else now... in *some* form. Or at least, he was."

"Why put these illusions to keep us in Windlyn Vale?" Atul said, having trouble with the words.

"I don't fully understand. But I know he fears our spreading across the world. It will thin his influence, dilute the enchantment over so much space. Perhaps we will fade too. He fears losing track of his favorite pets. So, he implanted lore into our minds as a leash, and barriers of illusion as our cage. It was only through my memory of him that I have overcome the power of the implantation to retain the truth. One that I've kept to myself for all these years."

"How do you, alone, know so much about our creator?" Siv asked, his head reeling.

"Jaerwin spoke to me before he succumbed to his madness and faded away. He told me of the aversion enchantment he placed at our borders. Like him, they are powerful. When you draw near his illusions, you wish to turn back without reason. Yet you accept it. You forget about it. I tested them long ago, and the effects were powerful, nearly killing me. He said he could tell me about his enchantments because, once the lore of the Calamity was implanted, it would take control and I would forget. But he didn't realize the strength of his own creations. He underestimated my resolve to keep the truth."

"This man, Jaerwin, created our kind, and you were the first?"

"No. The first was a nameless abomination. I am its

offspring, and the first to claw my way from the crust of the earth. I was the first broodling born in the Progeny Chamber."

"If what you say is true, then we are all your heir, and we are all of so-called common creation."

"Yes, the noble blood line is another fallacy. We can't all carry the burden of leadership, Siv. This division, arbitrary as it may be, has served its purpose.

"Creating division where there should be none is not a policy I would advise," said Siv.

"Then it was good that I put it in place well before your coronation, I suppose."

"And what happened to the first of the vilskje, the nameless abomination?"

"My mother was a mass of putrid flesh, arranged in horrific fashion. A genuine monstrosity. Yet, I could tell from her eyes she had self-awareness. One was on an appendage, and two others on one side of what might have been taken for a face. There was a sadness in those disjointed eyes, and a realization of what was to come. She wanted to live... I could feel it, but she couldn't express herself. But Jaerwin destroyed her, thinking our kind a mistake even after my birth. He sought to destroy me too, but I pleaded for my life—something my mother was not physically capable of doing. And he stayed his hand, then he was gone, faded. But," Wern said, his frame drooping even in his position on the floor, as if falling through the stone to a hell below. "He was right to want to destroy us."

"No," said Siv, shaking his head. "You were right to stay his hand. We have a rightful place in this world."

Wern shook his head slowly, his eyes locked on the seer.

"Siv, there's more." His voice was a pained whisper. "It's happening again. This was the third in a row. In the Progeny Chamber."

"Third what?" said Atul, bewildered.

Siv barely heard him. His mind had gone back to what he had overheard earlier that day. The weeping that came from that chamber as he walked the Council Hall from this same room. A shudder went through his body.

"Abomination," whispered Wern. "We had to destroy it."

Silence filled the room, each vilskje lost in his own thoughts.

Eventually, Wern spoke again. "I misspoke earlier. You are brilliant and wise, Siv. Your omen is true. And without knowing our past, you have uncovered it. I fear that Jaerwin's touch has faded after all this time and what remains has taken a dark turn to the perverse. Whatever correction he made at the time of my creation has uncorrected itself, it would seem. We unravel."

More silence followed until at last Wern spoke again. His voice held an uncharacteristic weakness. "I have not felt his presence for nearly three decades. I fear it's time to accept the truth. Jaerwin, our Father of Light, the Watcher —whichever you wish to call him—has abandoned us."

"No," said Siv. "It's not true."

"The animals of the vale fear us. They retreat when we draw near. But there are those that fear nothing, like the dire wolves, and they are not even the worst. There are creatures of this world that cannot tolerate the feeling. They will go to great lengths to destroy the source of their fear."

"Humans," said Siv.

Wern nodded.

Siv looked to the statue at the center of the room. The Father of Light was one of them, merely a man. He realized it didn't matter. For Jaerwin was no ordinary man—he was their creator.

Wern claims Jaerwin has abandoned us, but he's wrong. I've felt his love to this day.

Siv stepped closer, addressing the room in a bold voice. "Wern, you say that our creator, Jaerwin, is a man. Yet, in the same breath, you suggest the humans may destroy us. This is an interesting contradiction, to say the least. Perhaps our situation is not so easily diagnosed, Master. Perhaps the Watcher still watches."

Wern looked at Siv with consideration but said nothing.

"Put your trust in me," Siv continued. "And we will see this through."

Siv turned his head to see Atul smiling up at him, his eyes brimming with adoration.

The Watcher

Siv rode a wind current toward the shoreline in a daze. His head reeled from his meeting in the Council Chamber. He squinted, inhaling the salty wind deep into his gannet's lungs. Land became sea below and the sound of lightly crashing waves eased his nerves, if only a little.

The Father of Light... is a madman?

No matter how many times he repeated that thought, it wouldn't process. He swooped lower, instinctively moving where a fish breached the surface. He'd spent a long time in this dyr-form over the years, and what used to require concentration now happened automatically. The gannet's instincts had become his own.

Why would a madman guide me all these years? Why would he fill me with such warmth and hope in the darkest of times?

Something jumped out of the water in Siv's peripheral vision, and he spun right and dove, honing on silver scales. The herring made it less than half a foot beneath the surface before Siv sliced through the water like a spear, snagging the prey in his open beak. He turned up, eyes closed, sensing his way back to the surface, seeing the light of the sun brighten the darkness behind his eyelids. The herring squirmed in his beak and he salivated, enjoying the abrasion of its scales, relishing the salty taste and slimy texture.

Siv broke the surface, opening his eyes. He spread his wings and spun, shaking the sea from his feathers as he swallowed the fish whole, imminently satisfied. He banked right until he was parallel with the shoreline, now almost a quarter mile away.

Had he ever flown this far out before? He didn't even know. The diversion of the hunt fell away as quickly as it had come. He closed his eyes, inhaling deeply of the sea wind, and turned gradually back toward the shore. His mind returned to Jaerwin and the revelations from the council chamber. Wern had said their creator was fading away—he couldn't even feel Jaerwin's presence anymore. But that wouldn't be the case for Siv, would it? The thought of that guiding presence, whatever name it went by, vanishing from his life entirely was unbearable. But now that he knew the truth, would it happen to him?

Jaerwin, if you can hear me, give me a sign. I know your truth and... I don't care. I accept you. Please... I must know that you're still there. Please.

He opened his eyes.

At first he felt nothing, but slowly a warmth radiated in his feathered breast. It penetrated his heart and spread through his body, bringing him peace of mind. He would have smiled if his gannet form would allow it. An updraft lifted him and delivered him to the shore.

A message appeared in his mind, soft as a whisper. Not words, but an understanding. It didn't matter what Jaerwin was. He had created the vilskje, and he loved them. Siv swooped upward triumphantly, shrieking with joy and relief.

Human, deity, madman... it doesn't matter to me. Nothing has changed.

I will still call you the Watcher.

Siv swooped and landed at Holidae Cove. Here, the Zaqar river split into seven estuaries like narrow fingers reaching for the sea. He dyr-shifted to his fox and pranced along the fingers, eyes keen for mollusk or small crabs, hoping for another bite before he reached the meadow. He would take note of any activity near the forest line before returning to the burrow. He didn't want the clan to be caught off guard by any humans should they come through the forest.

He followed the fingers until they converged, disappointed at not finding a single crab along the way. Shrugging it off, he plunged into the tall grass, which rose above his red fur. He stalked west, keeping an astute ear to the wind. Every so often, he stood on his haunches to eye the perimeter of the woods before falling back down.

Halfway to the tree line, he heard something. So low he thought it his imagination until the ground vibrated beneath his paws. A rumble in the distance brought his gaze to the right, toward the burrow. He paused, transfixed. The clan moved toward him as one. The skin beneath his fox fur tingled with excitement.

How long has it been since the vilskje ran together through the vale?

Herd movement was a sporadic occurrence, and all vilskje were compelled to join the fray. Young vilskje without skill in the three requisite dyr-forms would stand and watch, pained at their exclusion. It would ignite their desire to develop, so they could take part in the next one.

The entranced faces of many wolves grew bigger as they neared his position by the river, carrying the rumbling with them. They would turn east before reaching him—the route was always the same.

Siv shifted to his wolf, hypnotized. This close to the ritual, his body was no longer his own. A thin, transparent membrane, unique to the ritual, slid over his eyes, filtering the colors of the world around him. The tall grass turned to golden spears and the sky a lavender veil. He took off, falling into place within the herd as it turned east toward the sea, now the richness of cobalt.

Those at the head of the ritual changed to deer on the move. They grew taller, their bodies thinning, their fur speckling and receding into skin which held its pattern. The soft rumbling turned to a thundering as nimble paws turned to hooves. Siv, without thought, shifted to his own vale deer. The herd at last reached the shoreline as ruminants, the sandy soil muffling the sound of their hooves. Crabs fled to the shallows and gulls dispersed, crying out as they flew to sea.

They cut north, running alongside Mount Svernos. Halfway to Galdhopiggen Swamp, the herd fell beneath the grass as field mice, scurrying parallel to the shore, sticking to the edge of the grasslands on their route. Something nagged at the back of Siv's mind, like he had been doing something else—something important—before this ritual, but it was lost now. There was only this moment. Staying in form and step with the clan.

The herd sprouted the wings of the common meadowlark. They flew low over the grass as one bird, formidable and beautiful. They turned west before the swamp, passing Tevryk Falls and circling the mountain, back toward the burrow. His mind found enough space for independent thought, and in it, there was nothing but joy from this moment. Of simply existing.

This is a beautiful magic. Natural part of the world or not—we are not Jaerwin's mistake. We are his magnum opus.

The herd broke apart near the burrow, nakken-shifting and wandering in separate directions. The ritual membranes retracted from their eyes, allowing the natural color of the world in again.

Facing the burrow, Siv found himself thinking of the falls he had just flown past with the clan. Tevryk had always been the northern end of their world, but now he knew that border was false pretense. There had been what looked like a limitless expanse beyond the cliffs that lined the edge of Glimryn Forest. But what lay beyond the falls? Curiosity turned him northward, if only for a quick glance.

Still in nakken-form, Siv inspected the rock making up the basin of the falls, expecting another malleable illusion like the one that had been at the edge of the forest. Stick insects, like tiny reflections of himself, stood on their long hind legs lapping the spray. They moved away as he approached, scattering around the edges of the flat rocks and turning back to eye him warily, their heads protruding upward. He tapped his claw against the side of the cliff.

Hmmm... it's solid. If Jaerwin sought to keep us contained in Windlyn Vale for some unknown purpose, wouldn't he have set an illusion here too?

Siv took a step back, looking high to where mist propagated above the crashing water.

Perhaps up there, above the falls?

Water sprayed his face and he tried to remember if he'd ever been here, where the falls crashed down to form the Zaqar River. In all these years, he didn't think so. Yet he had been close many times. The aversion must have been so subtle that it didn't feel a violation. He didn't even realize that it had spun him around and sent him walking back the way he'd come. It was as if he'd wanted to go that way in the first place.

It's only as I stand here in the cool mist of the falls that I even realize it... but why don't I feel the need to turn back now?

He frowned. It had to all be connected—the spell was weak here because the forest barrier had been breached. The humans may have torn it again from their side after we left, destroying it altogether. The dire wolves likely started it. They tore through, perhaps recognizing it as false by instinct. Their breach must have weakened it just enough to allow me to reach it through the forest. We've torn it twice since then. How many times can it possibly regenerate?

It was starting to make sense. Perhaps the illusion had been here before, and now it is gone. Or it may be higher up at the top of the falls.

Only one way to find out.

Siv shifted to his gannet and launched himself into the air, steering clear of the powerful crashing water. He flapped his wings furiously, dancing in the air all around the falls as he rose higher and higher toward the top. The cliffs at Tevryk Falls were high—taller even than Glimryn's towering trees. Siv's wings grew tired long before he reached the top, but he wouldn't stop until he saw what lay beyond.

"Siv! Where are you going?" a familiar voice shouted from below.

Startled, Siv looked down to see Atul standing at the base of the falls, where he had been only moments ago.

"Atul?" he shouted down.

"I followed you! It was curious how you just took off for the falls. What are you doing?"

"Nothing. I'm just looking up here and then coming right down!" Siv shouted.

Atul said nothing and Siv turned his attention back upward.

He was more than halfway when Atul shouted again, quivering with excitement. "I've found something! Here, behind the falls. If you look closely, there's a platform. You can only see it from a certain angle—I nearly missed it."

Siv's heart jumped in his throat. His wings stalled and he began to fall. He remembered what the pixie, Drexel, had told him. That there was an entrance to the dragon's lair behind the falls. Siv had sworn an oath of secrecy, but he had led Atul right to Laguznal's doorstep.

Atul inched closer to the edge. "If I hug the cliff, I could squeeze through and—"

Siv shouted. "Wait—Atul! You can't go in there."

Atul looked up at Siv, who came to land beside him, panting. "What? Why not?" he said.

"It's not safe," Siv insisted.

Atul glanced around. He looked to one side before settling on Siv again. "Well, what's in there?"

"It's, uh—"

Siv was cut off by a sound like thunder, followed by screams. There was a popping and more screams. Then there was a rumble which grew in the distance.

"That's coming from the burrow. Come, Atul. We must go back!"

First Contact

A slew of bodies stretched across the meadow outside the burrow. Open wounds red with blood were visible across the necks and chests of the victims, recognizable as humans. The sight reminded Siv of what the dire wolves had done to Perillia at the edge of the forest. But he knew dire wolves hadn't done this. It was the clan.

A scout confirmed his thoughts, racing across the meadow to recount what had happened. It had all happened in the brief time Siv had been at the falls. The humans had emerged from the tree line and marched across the grasslands, investigating what was a new territory to them. The men had killed one of the vilskje in dyr-form—Siv couldn't get a straight answer as to which animal—prompting a full-on retaliation from the clan. At first, Siv had thought this a one-sided affair, only seeing the human bodies laid out in the grass, but the scout shook his head.

"Many more of our clan were killed. Two or three of us for each one of them."

Siv paused, but then nodded.

Of course. The clan bodies were surely brought inside for Renewal. Wern would be taking them to the sacred ground now, deep inside the burrow.

"Some of the men had spears," continued the scout, "and we overcame them as our wolves. But others carried *those*." He pointed to a weapon laying on the ground beside a man's open hand. "Those spit something out at such speed it penetrates the flesh, killing instantly. It happens so fast, you can hardly see it. We stood no chance against the men with those weapons—only killed two of them."

"What made them turn back, then?" Atul asked, frowning. "I don't see any left here, unless they got inside the burrow. Did they?"

"No," said the scout. "Strigo turned the battle. He was in his chamber when this first happened, but when he came out of the burrow as his brown bear, it was like the humans lost their wits at the sight of him. He charged the two at the front of their group, knocking them down like swamp reeds so the wolves could finish them off." He pointed to a particularly bloody mess of a casualty. "Then he mauled this one really bad. I have never seen Strigo like that. Never."

"After that," said Siv, "the rest fled?"

"Yes. They were terrified. Strigo made a nasty mess of several others who tried to flee, chasing them down, biting and mauling them." The scout looked out over the field and pointed to a giant brown mass in the distance. "He's still out there, patrolling. The humans have retreated for now, but our air-born scouts report that more reside just inside the edge of the forest, waiting."

Siv nodded, processing.

"You should go inside. The clan is reeling from this, Seer."

"Our dead... they've been brought in for Renewal, I presume?"

"Yes, but... well you should go see for yourself." The scout averted his eyes and then turned back to his task of collecting the fallen men's weapons.

Siv glanced around at the carnage. His legs felt weak and hollow, like thin bamboo that may snap under his weight and send him crashing to the ground.

"Siv," Ilyana whispered. She had walked up from behind and now stood beside him.

He gazed up at her and knew that the graveness in her dark eyes must mirror his own. She lowered herself, hovering just above the ground, the vilskje posture of dread. A position that, he realized now, he himself was also in.

"Why do we have to first meet them like this... in death?" she said, her eyes vacant. "This is not how they seemed on the other side, roasting, laughing. These do not seem like the same things at all."

"No," he mumbled, his thoughts in a different place. The mens' eyes were frozen open, blankly looking up at the blue sky, seeing none of the beauty before them. He stared at them, transfixed. "I have met one before."

The Watcher.

Voices carried over from the burrow, bringing their attention that way. The trio made their way over and went inside. Spears lowered to meet them as soon as they entered, then relaxed as they recognized them as vilskje. Guards were huddled on either side, inside the entrance doorway. Their nerves looked to be on a razor's edge after the attack.

Normally Chief Protector Yuryk would station with his men, but he was not with them now.

The entrance chamber was mostly quiet, and one of the guards informed Siv that much of the clan had descended the winding tunnels to their personal chambers, where they would rest until they received word that it was safe.

Siv stepped past the guards, looking for the source of the despairing voices that had drawn them in. He soon found it. A group of elders stood huddled off to one side of the central bonfire, surrounding something. As he approached, Siv realized what the area of interest was. The bodies of the fallen vilskje covered a large section of the floor, laid out neatly in rows. One elder's tear sac burst, spraying fluid onto the bodies, and several others were close to doing the same. Others had angry faces with low postures and narrowed eyes. Their antenna nubs twitched, and their legs quivered. Most whispered or spoke gently. Some raised their voices in anger.

"Why hasn't the master taken them for Renewal?" said Delagria, a kind-hearted elder of common creation. "They are so many."

A tall one with eyes set wide apart seconded the notion in a pained voice. "This isn't right. Where is Wern?"

Siv raked a claw lightly down the side of his face, allowing each of the six digits to bring slight pain.

The elders' concerns are warranted. Why does no one come for the bodies?

This goes against centuries of custom.

Siv turned to face Delagria, whom he knew well. "These souls fought bravely for all of us today. To protect our clan.

They deserve Renewal. I will take this up with Wern and the Council immedia—"

A scream rang out like a sharp whistle from the group, cutting his words off. Instinctively, his gaze fell to the bodies. The red-orange light of the bonfire could now be seen *through* them. Soon, the horror of what was happening sunk in, and the elders cried and wailed until the floor was slippery with their tears.

Siv's mouth hung open. Ilyana's eyes were wider than he had ever seen.

The fallen vilskje were fading away.

They were disappearing.

Master Yuryk

Siv stepped into the Council Chamber, disgusted by what had just transpired. Seeing twenty or more of his fallen brethren vanish was not something he had been prepared for. There would be no Renewal for them. This was a brutal kind of finality that he wasn't used to. The vilskje lived incredibly long lives, relative to the other creatures of Windlyn Vale at least, and then the cycle began over again with the Renewal. But for their lives to just end like this, and so many. It was hard to fathom.

Ilyana followed him into the room. Somewhere along the way, he had lost Atul, he just now noticed. Atul had probably retired to his personal chamber, struggling as Siv had with what had happened to the bodies. He didn't blame him.

There was only one vilskje in the Council Chamber, crouched, with his back to them as they entered the room. He turned his head to one side upon their approach, staring at them from the corner of one eye. Then he stood and faced them.

It was Yuryk, chief protector. He stepped to one side, revealing Master Wern behind him. The master lay slumped in his engravement, his lifeless head hanging at the end of his neck.

Siv's skin crawled.

"Wern," Ilyana whispered, her mouth dropping open.

Yuryk's gaze fell in sullen reverence. He gestured to the master with two arms. "He did it right in front of me. I tried to console him, but..." The guard's voice cracked, frail as a dry leaf underfoot. "He ended his life, just like that." Yuryk shifted an elbow in its joint, making a cracking sound.

Siv walked closer, heart pounding, Ilyana shadowing him. He looked around the empty room. "Where are the other council members?"

"Wern ordered them away. He told them to come back only if they felt Jaerwin's presence. The master went mad, Seer, just like our creator. It's been happening slowly over the years. But today... I refused to leave his side, but I couldn't stop him. Now he's gone, and I've no choice but to assume his role."

"Why were you all cowering here while a battle raged in the meadows?" said Siv, raising his voice. "Why didn't you bring the fallen to the Sacred Chamber?"

Siv took a step closer, noticing what looked like red markings on Wern's neck. He didn't think those had been there before, but he couldn't be sure. A chill ran down his back and he locked eyes with Yuryk. "You say that he took his own life?"

Yuryk nodded. "He mentioned your omen... said it was over for all of us. Our kind."

"Look!" Ilyana said. "He's fading like the others."

Yuryk nodded. "You asked about the Sacred Chamber. That is yet another of Wern's fabrications. Our kind all fade when we die. It's all a show for the common bloods… which is of course, another lie. Layers upon layers."

Siv and Ilyana stood silent, mouths open. They shared a troubled glance.

"I served Wern faithfully for all these years, but I never agreed with these lies," continued Yuryk. "Well, no more." He clutched his shark-tooth spear tightly.

"This is a matter of discussion for later, Yuryk. Wern was master for a millennium and the first of our kind. There is no succession plan."

Yuryk turned away, his muscles looked more tense.

"Anyway, there are more pressing matters, right now," Siv said. "Our clan has been attacked by men from beyond Windlyn Vale. The very ones I warned you and Wern about, you might recall."

Yuryk sighed. "I know what has transpired, Seer."

Siv reached out and clasped Yuryk's arm, shaking it. "Listen! Things are far worse than I imagined. They have weapons that put them at an advantage, but we have killed many of them. That means they will seek retribution. Don't you understand? Their numbers are far greater than ours, Yuryk. They will come back—and there will be blood. I think they are settlers. They won't stop until this is their home. We could try to coexist, I suppose, but this is a rough start."

Yuryk scowled, pulling his arm back. "So, what do you propose? We flee like rats?"

Siv took a deep breath. He was getting irritated. Talking

to Yuryk was like entertaining a broodling. "Windlyn Vale is our home, but we should consider the fact that we may need to leave. Just in case... I've sourced an exit route over Tevryk Falls."

"We stay and fight." said Yuryk. "We won't bow down to the first enemy at our door."

Siv shook his head. "The vale is a fraction of the larger world. We can find a new home. I'm only saying we leave as a last resort."

"Fine. Keep your backup plan. But we will set our defenses. I will station a watch atop the burrow."

"Our greatest defense is Strigo. His brown bear saved the clan today by scaring them away. But they will be back. And when they come, they will target and kill him with their weapons, and his blood will be on your hands, *Master.*"

With that, he turned and left the room, gesturing for Ilyana to follow.

Outside in the hall, Ilyana sighed, shaking her head. "If Yuryk was so against Wern's secrecy, why did he do his bidding for a thousand years? I also find the master's passing suspect."

"I agree," said Siv. "And I have a bad feeling that the worst is yet to come."

ATUL THE APPREHENSIVE

Atul lay in the grass bed of his chamber. His mouth was raw from grinding his mandible from side to side. More than anything, he wanted to be out there with his mentor, Siv, helping with this situation. Proving himself. He wasn't meant to be a recluse, like some insect tucked beneath a rock, but he couldn't bear to be around them anymore. He was questioning everything.

Master Wern had proven unworthy of the clan's trust. He had held secrets from the entire clan—big secrets—for his entire time as master. His entire life. Atul had heard that from the master's own mouth. Yet, he still sat at the head of the clan with no repercussion.

Was Siv really any different? Atul would have never considered such a thing. As next in line for seer, Atul *adored* the current one. Siv was one of the best of the entire clan—reasonable and wise. Kind and understanding. Yet, the seer was clearly keeping secrets from Atul. At a minimum, he was excluding him from things. It was bad enough that the Council did not give him respect, but for Siv to keep things from him as well...

He spends all his time with Ilyana. Why is that? He only ever seeks me out when it's convenient, or he happens upon me. As next in line, he should want me at his side, always.

Feeling restless, Atul sprang to his feet. When he turned to face the entrance to his room, a hideous thought swept through his head like a toxic mist.

Maybe, instead of me, Siv wants Ilyana as the next seer.

The thought made Atul's blood boil. Perhaps Siv had wanted this for a long time, but he was too cowardly to tell him. Of course, the idea had never been a real concern before because Atul was next in line due to his Council blood. But that was just another of Wern's lies.

There is no Council blood... and no common creation. We are all the same.

There's nothing special about me at all.

He lowered himself close to the ground and narrowed his eyes, feeling the anger morph into something even more insidious. After a while, he took a deep breath and closed his eyes, trying to calm himself. Assuring himself that he was only being a fool again.

But then he remembered the entrance he had found behind the falls. Siv had stopped him from entering. Thinking back, Atul realized he'd never gotten a real explanation as to what was inside. Would Siv have stopped Ilyana from going in?

No. I don't think he would. In fact, he's probably told her about it. Maybe even brought her inside.

Atul straightened up, fully extending his legs. Taking

another deep breath, he walked out of his room and into the winding hallway toward the entrance. It was time to confront his mentor.

STRIGO THE STALWART

Siv stood with Ilyana at his side, peering out the burrow at the vast expanse of meadow bordered by Glimryn Forest to the south and west, and the Spyrul Sea to the east. The fingers of Holidae Cove, tributaries to the sea, lay hidden behind a gradual hill leading up before descending to the coast. Behind them, some of the vilskje had returned from their chambers, restless for news on what was happening. They bunched behind the two of them, but none asked to leave the burrow.

A brown object appeared in the distance, growing in size until it was recognizable as a brown bear.

"Strigo approaches," Siv said.

Ilyana nodded. "I'm surprised they haven't attacked him. Do you think the humans have retreated for good?"

Siv shook his head. "No. I think, like us, they are planning for the next move."

Strigo lumbered toward them with the graceless but incredible speed of a grizzly, and soon he was before them, panting and huffing, his foul breath causing Siv and Ilyana to grimace and turn away, gagging.

"They cower, Seer," roared the bear. "They have fled the edge of the forest too. Our birds confirm the same."

"You have done well, today, Strigo. The clan should honor your name."

Strigo fell to his knees, lowering his head. He shifted to his vilskje form, an elongated stick-insect form just a little longer and taller than the rest. Most thought his greatest gift was his physical prowess. But Siv knew that it was his spirit, pure and true.

"Rise, Strigo. You don't belong on your knees. Come with me to the burrow."

The bear-shifter followed his command, and the three turned and walked inside.

Inside the burrow, the elders had left their earlier place and the floor now lay bare where the fallen vilskje had been. The chamber was barren aside from guards on either side of the entrance. Yet several vilskje clung near the entrance to the common and Council Hallways, their beady eyes watching the three as they entered.

One of the vilskje recognized Siv and spoke. "Seer, are we safe?"

Siv walked deeper into the room, close to the bonfire. He let its warmth give him comfort, watched the smoke curl from the tips of its flames and spiral out of the hollows in the rock to the outside air. "No," he said at last. "I wouldn't use that word. They have retreated for now, but we don't know if they will come back. I will say this. I have seen their clan and they are many. They outnumber us."

"So, we're not safe?" asked another, younger vilskje, this one from the Council Hallway.

"I've prepared an evacuation route," said Siv. "As a last resort, in case we need to leave the burrow. The chances we may need it are greater than I would like."

Another vilskje shouted. "What do you mean, leave the vale? There is nowhere else!"

At this point, the vilskje began to slowly emerge from the hallways, filling in the entrance chamber, eyes on Siv.

"It's time you knew the truth," said Siv. "There is an entire world beyond the borders of Windlyn Vale. The Calamity is a fabrication."

The crowd gasped; they shuffled in discontent.

"Seer?" asked Strigo at his side. "Why are you saying this? Surely, it isn't true."

Siv turned to the stalwart, nearly a foot taller than himself. He placed an arm on his shoulder. "It's true Strigo. Ours is but a small part of the world. Help us survive and I will show you."

"Blasphemy!" yelled one vilskje.

Ilyana stepped forward. "Where do you think the humans came from?" she shouted angrily. "There is land beyond ours. I've seen it with my own eyes!"

"The humans might come back," said Siv, not giving the crowd a chance to interrupt. "They outnumber us. I'm not asking you to do anything right now beyond understand my words. But know that I have a plan," said Siv. "If things become dire, I ask that you follow me. Will you trust me?"

A familiar voice rang out from the Council Hall. "Trust

you? I'm not sure that I can, Siv. Can any of us truly trust you?" Atul stepped into the firelight.

Ilyana turned to him with surprise. "Atul? Is that you? After all Siv has done for you? How could you say that?"

Atul scowled. "After all I've done for *him*, you mean? He's always putting the final touches on my work. Who do you think lured the dire wolves to the summit of Mount Svernos in the first place? Who drove the leader off the cliff, killing him? It was *me*. What have you done, Ilyana, to be worthy of seer? Nothing."

Siv put an arm in front of Ilyana, holding her back. "Atul, I don't know where this is coming from, but Ilyana has no ambition of becoming seer."

"Lies! I know you keep secrets from me, Siv! Tell me then, what's behind the falls? Will you tell me that at least? I'll bet Ilyana knows."

Ilyana turned to Siv, confused.

Strigo jumped in the middle of the room, eyeing Atul callously. "I'd watch yourself, young one."

"Strigo, ease up," said Siv. "Atul, let's talk in private. Clearly there is a misunderstanding between us. No need to get the whole burrow riled up at a time like this. Come, let's walk to your chamber and discuss."

Atul said nothing, but Strigo stepped back, turning to the meadow again as if eager to shift to his brown bear once more.

Siv stepped past several vilskje and came up beside Atul. A moment later, the two were walking side by side down the Council Hall.

"Tell me, what is this all about, Atul?"

In the isolation of just the two of them, Atul seemed

less confident. "It feels like you are keeping things from me, Seer. You spend all you time with Ilyana, for one thing."

"Ilyana is a good friend of mine. We've always had a unique connection. But that doesn't diminish the relationship you and I share. We drove the dire wolves from Windlyn Vale. We stopped the wildfires in Glimryn Forest three years back... you and I."

Atul looked down, the tear sacs at the corners of his eyes filling with fluid. "I... I'm not sure what's come over me. I always have this feeling like I'm not good enough. Like I can never meet expectations. I always try so hard, but it's like I'm a failure. To the Council, and to you. It's starting to mess with me."

Siv placed a claw on Atul's shoulder. "You're far from a failure, Atul. You slayed the leader of the dire wolves. No one else can say that."

Slowly, Atul started nodding his head. At last he looked up and met Siv's eyes.

"Why don't you get some rest, and we can talk in the morning?" Siv said.

"Okay, Seer."

Siv nodded, patting his mentee on the back, and then he turned away, walking back the way they had come.

"Siv?" Atul asked from behind.

"Yes?" Siv turned to face the boy.

"Can you at least tell me what's behind the falls? You know... that cave I found today?

Siv felt a vein in his neck twitch. "Well, that's..." His voice trailed off, lost.

He should have been able to come up with something,

anything. But his mind was blank. "Let's just talk about in the morning, okay?"

"Yeah, okay," said Atul.

And something in the tone of Atul's voice made Siv's stomach churn.

ATUL THE FEARLESS

Atul reached out, letting the water crash over his claw and run down his arm. He gazed south, back toward the burrow, though he couldn't see it in the dark of night. Off to the left, Mount Svernos loomed large in the distance. The humid air so close to the swamp made it hard to breathe, but here, close to the falls, a cool draft mixed in.

What is Siv hiding here behind Tevryk Falls that he won't tell me?

He brought his gaze to the rock platform just behind the falls, barely visible in the moonlight. He took a deep breath and leapt across, landing on all six limbs and sliding on the smooth, wet surface. He stood before a giant, rounded entrance, a massive wormhole bored through the cliffs. A vile stench hung about here, and Atul disengaged his olfactory nub in disgust.

Atul glanced around as he crept inside the cave, suddenly feeling less than heroic in this place. He considered dyr-shifting to his vole for discretion, but he was already small in the tunnel's vastness. He looked back out one last time. A bushel of stick insects stood together at the edge of the platform, leaning creepily toward him, lapping the spray from the falls. Their beady eyes were dead set on him with a curious gaze as they quenched their undying thirst.

He shook his head and turned back to the giant wormhole. This was no time for cowardice. He had a feeling he was stumbling on something of great importance. This would be a story for the ages. Some great secret that he wasn't supposed to know. Why? Did Siv think he wasn't good enough? He was the one who had slain the leader of the dire wolves, while the seer hid in a bush.

He pictured the vilskje sitting around a bonfire, telling his story. How, those many years ago, Atul the Selfless took destiny in his own hands. How he discovered the greatest treasure of Windlyn Vale, hidden by Jaerwin's magic and hoarded by the seer. Who would have suspected the lowly Atul to discover it? How brave he was to venture behind the falls in the dead of night!

He paused, his daydream melting away. Something wasn't right. He scratched the side of his face until he figured it out. It was the moniker.

'Atul, the Selfless' doesn't fit this story. It's not bold enough.

Perhaps 'Atul, the Fearless' instead.

Yes.

Satisfied, he pressed on.

The giant wormhole wove to the right and the path sloped to a steep descent. He noticed a rumbling growing louder with each step along the way. The crashing waters of the falls must have masked the sound outside. Halfway down, he released the hold of his nostrils. He immediately sputtered into a coughing fit, the thick stench catching in his throat. It was even stronger here. Finally, he regained his composure and, willing his nasal cavity closed again, continued down until he reached the bottom.

Here, the rock floor turned to mud and mosquitos buzzed in his auditory orifice. He felt a sharp pain on his skin, and he swatted at the mosquito with an angry claw. Water leaked from the swamp above here and there, the drips finding pools of water somewhere in the darkness ahead. The rumbling grew louder. The path wound to the right and he followed it.

He froze.

Ahead, the path opened into a cavern and at its center lay a reptile so great it filled the space from ground to ceiling. It was the likes of which he'd never even considered as possible in this world. It was like the sea itself. Twisted, krill-like whiskers sprang from the sides of its snout, swimming in the darkness. Its cetacean blue scales, patterned like waves, crashed over its immense body. Its chest rose and fell with each rumbling breath, nearly shaking the walls of the cavern. Atul's own breath came in short, sudden gasps. He realized then that any semblance of hero he may have had within himself had run away, out of the wormhole and left the real Atul behind, paralyzed by fear. An insect in front of a God.

Watcher, help me. This was a grave mistake.

He took a deep breath and closed his eyes, regaining his sense.

I can slip away safely. It hasn't seen me. It sleeps.

The next moment, Atul had spun around and was walking back. He should never have come here. It was dangerous. Reckless.

Worst of all, he had betrayed Siv's trust.

But as he started up the slope, a voice chided him. High-pitched and new, like a broodling's first words after emergence.

Atul, the weakling. Atul, the coward.

The broodling laughed.

He pictured a group of young vilskje gathered around the bonfire. Only this time, instead of proclaiming his greatness, they simply laughed and laughed until they nearly burst. They rolled around in the dirt, slapping their claws on the ground and clutching their midsections as if to stop their guts from exploding.

Atul put his claws over his antennae nubs. "Stop. Go away," he said out loud, instantly regretting it as his voice echoed in the silence of the cavern. He turned around to see the reptile, still in view. It didn't appear to have heard him.

Phew... I won't make that mistake again.

But as he turned and crept away again, his claws clacking on the stone, creating a soft echo like raindrops on open water, the rhythmic rumbling behind him stopped and started again, this time louder, perturbed. There was a sound like a whale shooting water from its blowhole, and the cave shook.

No... no... Watcher please don't let it wake...

A sound of breath brought Atul's head around to see and he locked eyes with the great lizard, and at that moment he remembered the proper word for it. It was something that was only supposed to be in Siv's Tome, or tales around the bonfire. Something that never existed or had been destroyed in the Calamity. It was not something that should here in Windlyn Vale. A dragon.

"Don't go in there. It's not safe," Siv had said. *Oh, Atul, you fool.*

There was no kinship in its eyes. Those diamond vessels held at once the beauty of the ocean and, in a central tempest of the deepest red, a burning hatred so vast as to appear greater than the beast itself.

The dragon lifted its head to the ceiling. The deafening sound of its roar shook the cave, and likely all of Windlyn Vale. The space in front of its maw blurred from its scream. What had been slow drips from the ceiling now gushed water, new fissures forming from the quake. Atul stumbled, losing his balance and nearly falling. He caught sight of a smaller tunnel above and behind the dragon to one side, beside which a dead-end hollow appeared in the wall.

Somehow, his muscles loosened enough for him to turn and leap back around the corner the way he had come. He slipped on a wet patch in the smooth rock, and panicked, scuttling his feet in a manic run up the slope. Behind him, the dragon roared again, the sound deafening.

There was a crackling and a hiss and then Atul's back and legs were burning. He screamed and turned his head to see orange and red tongues of flame licking his body. He crashed down on the slope, rolling and screaming. The flames vanished, leaving the path filled with steam and smoke in the humid air. Intense pain radiated through his body. He groaned and scrambled to his feet as fast as he could, panicked. Suddenly, nothing mattered except escaping those flames. Behind him came a huffing sound, like that of a thousand grizzlies on the hunt, and he darted up the slope, focusing on the sound of the crashing water ahead.

Near the top, he turned back to see two raging eyes where he had just been, visible now where the smoke had thinned. An enormous claw appeared and pulled the dragon up the slope until its entire head was visible through the smoke. Its whiskers twitched as it slithered toward him.

Awake

Siv woke to distant thunder. He shot up in his chamber and sprang to his feet. He stood for a second, listening intently. There was no more thunder and no rain pounding on the top of the burrow. Questions flooded his mind.

Are the humans back?

No shouts broke the night's silence. There were no screams of death. He ran outside his chamber, his claws clattering on the stone. He heard rustling in chambers as he ran past. Others had heard the rumbling as well.

Was it just another storm?

"Seer?" a voice came from behind. "What was that noise?"

He turned back to see a pair of tiny shining eyes, like onyx in starlight. One of the youth vilskje. There were more shuffling sounds, and another poked its head out of its chamber, like the prairie dogs which breached the meadows north of Holidae Cove.

"I'm not sure. Stay here until I return," Siv said then

turned away, moving faster than before until he reached the entrance chamber. The central bonfire cast immense light, shining onto many pairs of eyes, cowering at the entrance to the Council Hall on the other side. He glanced back to see that a crowd of vilskje had gathered behind him now. Their eyes were high and low, and to either side as they huddled around each other, all wanting to see, none daring to move further. They looked to Siv like one amorphous creature, slinking in the dark.

Abomination.

The last conversation with Wern stuck in his mind. Something was wrong with the new creations. Something was wrong with *them.*

Abomination.

Another sound came from the distance, this one so loud that it shook the burrow.

That's not thunder. It comes from the north.

A realization struck Siv so hard as to set him trembling. He lowered his body to the ground, feeling chills soar down his spine. The sacs at the corners of his eyes filled, ready to burst in tears of anguish at this thought which must not be true.

"Siv!" shouted a familiar voice. It was Ilyana. She stood at the door, her concerned face aglow from the light of the central bonfire. "Where's Atul? He's not in his chamber. And what is that noise?"

A chill went down Siv's spine as he surmised what had happened. Atul had gone behind the falls. He had thought Siv was hiding something from him, and he went to see.

No, Atul... tell me you didn't. Please...

Siv shook his head, panic coursing through his body.

From the entrance, Siv turned back to face the clan. What seemed like a hundred scared faces peeked out from the general and council quarters.

"Stay here. All of you."

He turned to Ilyana. "Come with me. I'll explain on the way."

Siv and Ilyana dyr-shifted and took to the sky. She followed his lead, pulling sharply up and banking left toward the falls. "What is going on?" she shouted.

"There's a dragon in Windlyn Falls—and Atul just woke it. We must save him."

"A dragon?" squawked Ilyana flapping her wings furiously. "You're serious?"

A deafening roar at the falls ahead answered her question and drew her attention. The wind howled and the mountain loomed like a giant to their right as they flew to their friend. They drew near just as Atul hobbled out from behind the falls. He was limping, in clear pain. He leapt to one side just as bright red fire burst from the cave, the powerful flame piercing the waterfall and shooting out into the night.

"Atul!" Siv and Ilyana both shouted.

The boy, still in the distance, didn't notice them. With difficulty, he dyr-shifted to his hawk. Finally, he launched into the air and flapped his wings mere seconds before the great dragon burst through the waterfall like lightning, stretching its magnificent wings in the moonlight. It released a booming roar, making Siv's head pound. He dove, nestling his head between his shoulders to mute the horrible sound. Ilyana made a similar desperate move.

Siv righted himself, swooping back into the air. About

15 yards from the falls, it was apparent that something was very wrong with Atul's hawk. The bird flapped and spun, diving right and then correcting left before falling and flapping furiously to stay in the air.

"He's hurt!" Ilyana said, her head tilted in the seer's direction.

"I'll draw it away!" Siv shouted.

The dragon was dead set on Atul, now. The boy had fallen to the sticky mud of the swamp, where he struggled to free himself in a panicked flurry, one wing stuck while the other flapped wildly. It was a sight familiar to Siv. He had been wedged in that same foul trap only days before, though there hadn't been a dragon at his back.

Atul craned his head toward the dragon above him, triumphant and glorious, its wings nearly half the span of Mount Svernos.

His desperate, screaming pleas were a pitiful, gut-wrenching sound. "Please... I'm sorry I disturbed you. I'm not your enemy!"

Atul's next words were lost as a great breath of fire burst through the night sky, lighting up the northern face of the mountain. The flame traveled over Atul's head all the way to the sea, and it looked to have burned Atul, for his screams filled the air. The dragon had shown no regard for his words. It was toying with its prey.

"Siv! Ilyana!" Atul screamed, apparently noticing them for the first time. "Please, help me!"

The dragon hovered, a pelagic god with scales like tidal waves. From the side where Siv swooped in, he could see its long whiskers, twisted like forks of lightning. Its eyes were orbs of red-centered malice, burning with hatred. The dragon flapped its giant wings, sending Siv sprawling backward toward the mountain. Waves swept the shallow swamp waters toward the sea. They lapped over Atul's body, choking out his pleas. The dragon lashed its tail back and forth with another deafening roar.

Siv spun back around to see Ilyana approaching the dragon. She screamed for its attention, but it was too late. The dragon shot its breath directly onto Atul, his hawk's feathers igniting, smoldering. He screamed, a high-pitched, pitiful sound.

At last, Ilyana caught the dragon's attention. She flapped her small thrush wings about its face, keeping at enough of a distance for a chance, should the dragon lash out at her. The dragon stopped its assault on Atul, who had nakken-shifted in his weakness. It let out an annoyed hiss and spun toward the bird.

Siv came back to Ilyana's side.

I must do something!

He flew in front of her, his gannet gaining the reptile's attention. He flapped his wings as the dragon's eyes followed his movement. "Come! Get me!" he screamed and then he dove and took off, flying as fast as he could for Mount Svernos. He didn't look back. He felt the subtle pull of the wind, letting his gannet instincts guide him to the optimal place in the current.

Please, Watcher, if you are still there, let the dragon follow me. Keep Ilyana safe.

Behind him, the beast roared and flapped its wings. Siv felt a glowing warmth in his feathered breast, the same feeling as he had the day before. He banked right, blindly.

Guide me, Jaerwin.

When he opened his eyes, he was approaching a notch in the northeastern face of the mountain. Without so much as a thought, he flew into the crevice, landing in a tumble of feathers and smacking into a wall inside the small hollow, dazed but uninjured. He shifted to his shrew to blend with the tight darkness of the space.

Not more than three seconds later, the dragon flew by, the wind from its wings driving him like a tempest flat against the back wall of the crevice. It circled, bellowing rage and spiteful fire upon the mountain side.

Atul was surely lost, a thought that filled him with a great sadness.

But Siv had given Ilyana a chance. Small as it may be.

Please, Ilyana. Get away, my friend. Hide.

Bogged Down

Ilyana flew down to Atul. The young vilskje, so bold and ambitious the day before, now twitched and moaned. His body smoked and, as she drew near, she could see how his breath labored. She nakken-shifted to land in the mud, sending water flying.

"I'm going to get help," she said, her voice trembling. "Can you move?" Remorse filled the sacs at the corners of her eyes, and one burst, its fluid spraying onto the rippling surface of the swamp water.

Atul's head moved slightly. His tiny eyes were charred black. "I... saw its eyes. They were evil. There was nothing else."

Ilyana stroked his arm with the smooth back of her claw.

"Don't touch me," he whispered. "Please, it hurts so bad."

The sac in Ilyana's other eye burst now, spraying wildly through the air. The skin of the first sac had reformed now. She could feel it fill again, this time with despair.

"I'll get help. Just hang on, Atul."

In the distance, the dragon roared.

"I would've made... an awful seer," muttered the boy, barely able to get his words out. "Only now, I realize that. But you, Ilyana..." He clutched her arm. "You're special," he whispered. A piece of soot slid off his eye, and he locked his gaze with her. "Siv needs you. They all do. Leave me."

Ilyana squeezed his claw with her own. A second later, she saw lifelessness in his one clear eye.

Soon, he'll fade out like he never existed.

Her eye sacs shot despair into the swamp, and the dragon roared again, closer this time. She dyr-shifted to her raccoon and ran as fast as she could to where the reeds grew thicker, her body trembling. She rolled in the mud like a feral hog and burrowed as deep as she could. She breathed slowly, willed herself invisible, imagining herself a swamp reed. She tried to calm herself, but it was a hard task, for she knew her skill at camouflage wouldn't matter if the dragon unleashed its flame on the swamp.

Watcher, if you're still there, protect me.

She felt wind from the dragon's wings and feared it might send the mud flying from her striped fur. Yet she stayed still, calming herself, correcting her panicked breaths.

The reeds will still provide cover. It won't see me.

The dragon roared, a deafening sound followed by a great cackling of flame. A second later, intense heat flashed on her back, and she clamped her eyes shut, grimacing in pain. She held her eyes closed, expecting to erupt in fire and agony, but it didn't happen. The dragon's breath had flown over her, she realized. The dragon roared again, this time with more intensity.

It's frustrated. It can't find me.

The ground shook again, knocking Ilyana on her side, where the reeds rubbed the remaining mud from her back. Her heart raced, and she opened one eye, only to be immediately blasted by fierce wind from the beast's wings. It didn't turn back as it flew east, out to the sea. She stared with wonder, mouth open, shocked that she survived the encounter.

Ilyana wasted no time. She sprang from the reeds and sprinted over the swamp mud on her adept raccoon claws toward the burrow. Once her feet found the stable soil of the meadow lands, she nakken-shifted on the move, gaining even further speed in her gallop to safety.

"Goodbye, Atul," she said as she ran, and the words overwhelmed her with sadness, though she wouldn't allow her muscles any slack in her fleeing. Her tear sacs, filled now with loss, burst, one, then the other, streaming fluid into the grass.

Battle of the Vale

So, they would come again in the night.

In his gannet form, Siv peered southwest through the moonlight from his notch in the mountain. In the distant vale below, humans—droves of them—marched northeast from the forest. He saw a similar, but smaller, force of vilskje emerging from the burrow to meet them. A brown figure, small in the distance, led the clan into battle, and Siv's keen gannet eyesight allowed him to surmise it was Strigo's brown bear.

"Cursed fools," he spat. "Do they not hear Laguznal?"

A feeling of urgency overwhelmed him. He needed to act *now*, but he didn't know what to do. The abyss dragon had flown back to the swamp, abandoning its search for him with a thunderous tantrum.

He could go back to help Ilyana. But she was resourceful. She was probably already hiding. Going back would needlessly put him in danger for little benefit. He'd already given her a chance to escape.

Instead, he should go aid the burrow. Perhaps he could help with a ceasefire or at least warn them of the dragon.

As if hearing his thoughts, Laguznal appeared from the darkness over the sea, flaunting its giant wings in a slow, rhythmic procession, surprising Siv and causing him to stumble backward in his crevice on the mountainside. He was about to shift back to his shrew when he noticed the dragon change direction. It wasn't coming his way, toward the mountain. Its attention was on something else.

Watcher, it sees them now. Down in the vale. Scatter, you fools!

The men were pointing up at the sky, now, toward the dragon. They didn't run, their disjointed movement showing confusion as to what they were actually seeing. The vilskje on the grasslands were oblivious, focused only on the approaching humans.

When Laguznal screamed this time, it was an angry, visceral scream. An ancient battle cry and a warning that could not be heeded, only witnessed briefly. The moonlit sky grew blurry before the abyss dragon, its territorial shriek bursting like waves through the atmosphere. The reptile fell swiftly toward the battle of men and vilskje.

At that same moment, a movement far below, small and swift to the east, caught Siv's attention. He did a double take, craning his gannet's neck and squinting. A vilskje ran to the burrow at full speed. It was the only one outside, and it ran *away from the swamp.*

"Ilyana!"

He launched himself from the ledge and dove, tracking his friend like he would a mackerel over the water. He matched her running speed to land, nakken-shifting into a run beside her, impressing himself at the precision of his own desperate action.

"Ilyana..."

She turned her head without breaking stride, her eyes filled with grief. He nodded, understanding. Atul was gone.

Up ahead, the dark sky turned a fiery red and the screams of burning men and vilskje filled the night. The awful sound wove a dread needle through his heart. The hopelessness a prey animal must feel when a predator rakes its nails down its back. When it feels itself weakening and knows it can't escape.

"The tome is clear on dragons," Siv said, huffing for breath. "They never stop hunting. Not until everything around them is dead."

Sole Survivor

The vilskje huddled inside the burrow, peering outside. Their tiny eyes absorbed the carnage with fright and confusion.

Few recognized the creature that flew over the vale spewing fire.

Even fewer could decide whether to be grateful or terrified.

Most, from the look in their eyes, felt an unsettling combination of the two.

It was clear to all that the humans had planned to attack the burrow that night. In retribution for their losses, or in the simple spirit of conquest—they couldn't know. And yet, the vilskje that had bravely received them on the battle-field had not been met with honor, only the scorching fire of this unholy lizard.

The screams held steady. Laguznal had circled back once, flanking their forces from the south with new fire, then it came at them from the forest to the west, inciner-ating would-be survivors who fled to the cover of its trees.

Eventually, the dragon's breath consumed the forest itself, lighting it ablaze. Any man or vilskje lucky enough to avoid the hellfire was scooped up in the dragon's jaws and consumed whole.

The vilskje watched in horror from the burrow as their vale was reduced to barren ash. The humans were gone, vanquished entirely, it seemed, and the threat of their invasion died with them. But so were all the best vilskje warriors, the strongest that had gone to meet their would-be-oppressors, and the scouts who had served honorably as messengers. Nearly all had been caught in the fury of the dragon's flame.

As horrible as the scene was, the surviving vilskje felt relatively safe afterward. Surely, no human would dare step foot in the vale again. And the massive dragon, which still prowled the night sky, could not squeeze into their burrow, no matter how hard the terrifying beast may try. And so, one by one, the vilskje retreated to their chambers and slept. They were safe.

But one human had survived. A young man arrived at their entrance chamber the next morning. He crept from a sparse patch of grass like a beetle, black and grey with soot. Once on the barren ground, he sprang to his feet and sprinted, leaping quickly inside the burrow. He crouched there, breathing heavy, his head turning from side to side.

He was met by Council spears. Several of the vilskje from the general quarters joined them, dyr-shifting to grey wolves and baring their fangs.

Siv stood silent, observing, while Ilyana was alone in support of the young man.

"The dragon killed his entire clan before his eyes," she

said. "Now he cowers before us. All alone. Weaponless. Powerless. Are you all afraid? Let's hear what he has to say."

Yuryk approached the boy, locking eyes with him but speaking to the clan. "Two days ago, his kind killed more than twenty of our clan. Last night, more approached with weapons. If not for the dragon, they would have tried to slaughter us. He's not welcome here."

The new master's words garnered overwhelming approval from the clan and, despite an appeal from Siv to let him stay, they pushed him out. The guards turned the boy around and placed their spear tips at his back, pushing.

The boy sobbed. "Please, don't send me back out there with that thing. The scouting party made a terrible mistake. They were afraid. We've never seen your kind. Shape-shifting... it's just a myth. One fired his gun, but it was a mistake. We're not all like that. Please, let me prove it to you."

Yuryk ordered the Council guards to push him outside, where the boy got to his knees, weeping. He trembled with his hands on his face.

"Perhaps a little mercy," muttered the elder Delagria, hesitantly. Zurt nodded agreement by her side.

Siv approached Yuryk, pleading. "Don't do this, Yuryk. The boy shows remorse. The dragon will kill him, and we've seen enough death."

Yuryk pointed a bony finger at Siv. "I will *not* allow an enemy into our home."

He turned to the boy, who looked up at him with wet, frightened eyes. "Run there, boy," he pointed to a small section of the forest not yet burning. "You may just have a chance. If you make it, tell your kind to stay away. Now go!"

Yuryk gestured to the guards, who gave the boy a hard shove, knocking him sobbing into the dirt. "If you come back," said the smaller of the guards, "we'll kill you."

The boy scrambled to his feet, wiping his eyes. He looked all around, clearly trying to locate the dragon. He turned his head back one last time, and the desperate plea in his eyes broke Siv's heart.

This isn't right. He's just a boy. Is Jaerwin satisfied with his creations now?

Then, the boy was off, running as fast as he could toward the forest. He leapt over the burned bodies of his kind, pushing himself back to his feet where he stumbled, until he was nearly at the Zaqar river.

"We shouldn't have sent him back out there," said Ilyana, her voice laden with anger.

The forest was ablaze, except for a small section where the boy headed, just beyond the river.

Siv stepped outside the burrow, suddenly determined to help the boy. *I'm faster as my wolf, and he's small enough to ride on my back. Maybe I can hel—*

Laguznal's thunderous cry erupted from atop Mount Svernos and a strong wind spun the vale's ash into a whirlwind. The boy was just past the river's edge, near the forest, when the flame hit him, engulfing him from behind. His high-pitched scream was a terrible thing, a pitiful sound, and it tore Siv apart inside. He glanced at Ilyana as a sac of tear fluid burst from her eye. The boy fell to the grass, on fire and shrieking, before rolling into the river, silent at last, his lifeless body washing out to the sea.

Siv turned to glare at Yuryk, feeling hatred burning inside.

What have we become to sponsor this atrocity? No wonder our offspring turn monstrous.

He turned to Ilyana, his own voice laden with anger now. "Perhaps the red tide came to warn the world of *us*."

She met his gaze, her eyes filled with sorrow.

Outside, Laguznal roared. Siv brought his attention to the dragon. It stood at the center of the vale on its two back legs like a bear and breathed fire over the last unscathed section of trees. Now the entire forest was burning.

Siv glanced to once side, a dark realization setting in.

The dragon's not going back to its lair. Even after all this carnage.

Laguznal dropped on all four feet and craned his neck upward, sniffing the air, unbothered by the thick black smoke which billowed all around. He huffed, turning one way and then the other before taking to the air in a rage. He flew west over the flames of the forest toward Jaerwin's former illusion, those cliffs that had disappeared after all this time. Beyond that, Siv knew, was the humans' burrow above the ground, where the men, women and children had settled. He thought back to when he, Ilyana, and Atul had breached the illusion to observe them singing, playing games, roasting. Surely, they weren't all dangerous, but it didn't matter now. The dragon was coming.

Watcher, it's going to kill every single one of them.

He pictured the humans at play one moment and burning in the next, screaming and fleeing to their homes, only to realize that those too were on fire. A moment later, the vision faded away, replaced by real screams from the other side of the forest.

Intruder

Over the next two days, little changed in Windlyn Vale. The vilskje remained holed-up in their burrow. All the land south of Mount Svernos had been turned into an ashen wasteland, and the natural animals of the vale—deer, wolf, meerkat—were nowhere to be seen. They hid where they could, either underground in their burrows or in the sparse vegetation of the northern swamplands. Many fled the area altogether. If any humans even still drew breath—unlikely at best—they did not come back to their lands.

The dragon remained close. The vilskje rarely saw it from their south-facing burrow, but they could hear its screams, like fierce challenges in the wind. Every last one of them feared this hateful creature, which delivered a fiery death to every living thing in its path. It had not taken a side in their battle. Laguznal pledged allegiance to nothing but destruction. It had turned their beautiful forest barren and dark with its flame breath, the towering trees formerly lush with life now empty and black as night.

Siv prayed to the Watcher, encouraging others to do the same, hoping Jaerwin could somehow influence the fearsome reptile into giving them reprieve. But Laguznal didn't leave or alter its behavior. A period of silence brought them hope, but, soon after, a fierce flapping of wings kicked ash up from the ground like the driest of fogs until they could see nothing outside. The vilskje near the entrance choked and rubbed their burning eyes. Many retreated to the inner quarters of the burrow, but others remained up front, straining to see through the ash. Siv watched the entrance from just inside the Council Hall.

Suddenly, the ground shook and Laguznal's head appeared inside, bursting through the cloud of ash. The dragon snatched two vilskje in its jaws and pulled them outside, screaming. One shifted to a lark to escape, but the dragon jerked its head and chomped down, eating them both. The dragon vanished for a few seconds, only to come back even more determined, its head inside once more and now slamming its shoulders into the burrow, trying desperately to gain entrance. It screamed in frustration. The burrow shook and the vilskje prayed. How quickly their faith came back when the dragon unleashed its fiery breath, scorching many and sending others, Siv included, fleeing deep in their home.

The dragon breathed its fire into the burrow for several minutes. However, it could not squeeze its massive body inside, and its breath would not reach the deep innards of their burrow, which wound into the ground like intestines. Eventually, Laguznal retreated with a final, hateful scream. After the attack, the majority of the clan remained alive but traumatized, and they all shook like branch tips in the wind.

The next morning many migrated to the Council Chamber, ignoring their roles or placement in regard to the Council. Yuryk allowed them to gather around the statue of the Father of Light, where Siv led a prayer. To Siv's surprise, the vilskje still clung to their faith after the recent revelations about Jaerwin. There was nowhere else to turn, after all. News of Wern's death had passed through the clan now, and many cast hopeful glances at Siv, waiting for his answer to the dragon. After the prayer, Yuryk went to the entrance for updates from his guards and the remaining vilskje left the room, returning to their personal chambers.

Ilyana stayed behind to talk with Siv. "We can't hide in our burrow forever, Siv. What are we going to do?"

"I don't think the dragon will ever leave. The Great Tome defines them as territorial forces and this one's lair is right here in Galdhopiggen Swamp."

Ilyana sighed, looking frustrated. "Then what can we do?"

"We must leave, soon. I think we can escape over Tevryk Falls if we're careful. But there is one detail I still need to figure out. Have you seen Strigo? He wasn't at the prayer."

Ilyana shook her head and looked down.

Siv took her claw in his. "We will get to a better place, Ilyana. I know it. Just bear with me a little longer."

She met his eyes, nodding slowly. "I trust you, Siv."

After several minutes of walking around and asking his whereabouts, Siv finally found the stalwart Strigo. He was deep in the burrow beyond the vilskje's general quarters where the torches were few and the paths less clear. Many halls here led to dead ends, walls of packed earth serving no purpose. Somewhere deep in this section was rumored to be the Room Below, a repository reserved for those who commit crimes, or those of unsound mind. He wondered for the first time if that room was just another of Wern's fabrications. He had never seen it with his own eyes.

Strigo stood in a random hallway, leaning against a wall. The torchlight hardly touched him here, but Siv recognized him for his size alone. It was the reason why he needed to talk with him.

"Strigo, what brings you to these depths?" Siv called out as he approached. "I've been looking for you."

The stalwart straightened, stretching his legs as if he'd been leaning there for hours. "I come here sometimes, Seer. When I need solitude but don't want to be in my chamber. It feels more like a prison these days."

Siv stopped in front of Strigo, looking up at the giant shifter to meet his eyes. "That's what I wanted to talk with you about. I'm going to approach Yuryk with a plan to leave Windlyn Vale behind. I don't think this dragon will ever leave, Strigo. We must find a new place to call home."

The stalwart stood perfectly still and silent. Finally, Siv spoke again. "I need your help. How skilled are you at pocketing in your dyr-forms?"

"Skilled," said Strigo. "I don't have much need for it, but I have done it before."

Siv nodded. "Good. The clan doesn't have much in the way of material possessions, but there is one thing we must bring with us when we leave Windlyn Vale behind. The Great Tome."

There was another round of silence before Strigo spoke again. "You want me to carry your book beneath the flesh of my brown bear?"

Siv's jaw tightened at the question, noting a reluctance in the stalwart's tone.

"You have served the clan well these last few days, Strigo. Do this last task for me and I will ensure you a place at Council in our new home, wherever that may be. From now on, your voice will be heard."

At last Strigo responded, his voice deep and slow. "I accept your task, Seer."

Relief washed over Siv. "Thank you, Strigo. You are a true friend."

"I am only Strigo," he said. "If that is all, please return my solitude." At that he leaned against the wall again and closed his eyes.

"As you wish," Siv said, and he turned and left.

LAGUZNAL

That night, Siv approached Yuryk in the Council Chamber.

"I think it's time we accept the truth, Yuryk."

The new master leaned forward in his engravement in the stone floor, the one that used to belong to Wern. The space didn't fit his body quite right, but he did his best to conceal that fact. "That your underling poked around where he shouldn't have, waking a dragon, and cursing us all?"

"No. I was going to say something a little more... pragmatic," Siv said, brushing off the insult. "Our food stores are running out, and our last three attempts at gathering from outside left two dead and one badly scalded. Then, yesterday, the dragon killed several more of our clan when he tried to enter the burrow. Laguznal is not going away. He's toying with us."

Yuryk stood up. "What would you have me do?"

"Support my plan to leave Windlyn Vale. Staying here

means slowly starving. We should go north over Tevryk Falls."

"A mass exodus while that demon watches? That's your advice?"

"Each of us began our shifting lives with a slight form—field mouse, vole, or shrew. The clan will assume its rodent shapes, and we leave in the night. We'll follow a path north to the falls. There's still grass that way for us to hide beneath. The dragon won't see us. And when we're gone, he'll still think us in the burrow."

Yuryk frowned, considering. "That almost seems plausible." He turned to one side and paced, his claws clacking on the stone floor. "Once there, how do we get everyone to the top? Last time I checked, rodents don't swim up waterfalls."

"Leave that to me."

Eventually, Yuryk relented, unable to voice another option. Though he refused to rule out a return to the burrow, calling the plan tentative.

The next day, he pulled the clan together. Many were frightened, but all grew hungry and restless from being holed up in the burrow. The dragon seemed a permanent fixture atop the mountain, and the Windlyn Vale of old had withered into something far less in their minds. The lack of sunlight made their pale skin paler, and their worried minds turned to darker thoughts in its absence. By the end of the meeting, Siv had full agreement from the clan.

They left that night. Siv and Ilyana led the clan on one side, Yuryk and the other council members on the other. Elders, Zurt and Delagria, who insisted on seeing all to safety, covered the rear. All went as rodents, except for

Strigo, who clambered in the night as his brown bear, faithfully carrying the Great Tome inside his flesh. The clan moved slowly around the southeast face of the burrow then cut due north, shuffling nervously on their tiny feet beneath thickets and patches of grass. Strigo stuck close to the mountain side, away from the open grassland for fear of the dragon's gaze.

It started off without a hitch. The entire remaining clan —several hundred of them—crept toward the falls without so much as a stir from Laguznal. But soon they came to the place that Siv feared. It was a place he hadn't mentioned to Yuryk or anyone else, for fear of them not agreeing to his plan. Now, as he looked at the bald patch just ahead, perhaps ten yards across, he feared they would have been right. In this stretch of the land they would all be exposed.

Watcher, conceal us under the veil of night.

The group came to a halt at the edge of the grass, many no doubt feeling foolish for not recognizing this blemish in their seer's plan. Hundreds of eyes fell upon Siv, including faithful Ilyana, at his side.

They will only trust the plan if I go first.

He motioned with his shrew's paw for them to follow and turned his furry head toward the falls, now visible in the distance. He took off running across the gap, his beady eyes focused on nothing but the tall grass which rose like trees on the other side. He didn't need to look back to see his plan had worked. He could feel the padding of their feet on the ground behind him.

Siv made it to the other side, with Ilyana and Yuryk soon after. The tall reeds west of the swamp would provide sufficient cover from here on. Strigo had never stopped and was ahead of them all, racing across the swamp toward the falls. Siv's heart pounded as he scurried toward the falls. His plan was working.

We're nearly there! Maybe the gap wasn't such a—

The sound of giant flapping wings brought him to a sudden halt, and the others slid to a stop behind him. It was a sound he'd prayed not to hear. A second later, Laguznal roared. Siv lowered himself to the ground, uncertain of what to do. Yuryk and Ilyana mimicked his action, falling to the ground beneath the tall grass.

Siv turned around and looked to the night sky between blades of grass. The dragon circled above. Suddenly, flame shot from its mouth, the fire crackling and popping on the meadow behind them, closer to the burrow.

It missed the clan entirely. It doesn't know where we are.

Siv wanted to continue to the falls, but they wouldn't be able to emerge there while the dragon was aroused. Suddenly, Laguznal let out a deafening roar and changed direction toward the burrow.

A vilskje several feet back shouted. "Delagria has nakken-shifted! She's running back to the burrow!"

"Zurt too!" screamed another. "He's running after them!"

Another one said, "They're splitting up, now. He's running to the sea!"

"They give us a diversion!" shouted Siv and his heart swelled at the selflessness of the act. The sacs at the corners of his eyes began to fill with gratitude. He sprang up and shouted to the clan. "We must honor it!"

He took off running and the clan followed, northward through the striped reeds. It was slower going here, where the ground was damp and muddy so close to the swamp. Behind them the dragon screamed. Up ahead, Siv could see the glowing eyes of a brown bear behind the waterfall. Strigo had made it.

They were less than five yards from the base of the waterfall, when Laguznal screamed overhead and landed in front of Siv with such force that it shook the ground. The dragon faced them, blocking their path forward, steam rising from its mouth. It turned its head to the sky and roared, the sound hateful and victorious in equal measure.

It snapped its jaws in a show of dominance, the clacking of its teeth as loud as a tree slamming into the side of a mountain. Then it inhaled, its broad chest growing to tremendous scale.

Siv's heart slammed inside his tiny chest. He turned back to the clan and screamed, "Get out of its path, now! Run to the sides!" Without thinking, he bolted west toward the foothills, away from the swamp. Ilyana ran beside him. He could see some others doing the same, but most had turned straight back at the sight of the dragon and were fleeing for the burrow.

"Get out of its path!" Siv screamed, desperately. Ilyana joined in, screaming for them to listen. But in their panic the clan didn't hear them, and most were too far away now. A second later, Laguznal exhaled an unholy storm of fire onto the vale, straight at the fleeing rodents. The flame was thick and hungry, lapping up the grass and scorching the earth. It caught the vilskje in their losing race, feeding on them, setting them ablaze, their fur burning, their flesh melting, their eyes popping and sizzling. The clan screamed in collective anguish as hundreds died in agony on the grasslands of their home. As they perished, they nakken-shifted, their insectile bodies as charred black as the ground they had fallen upon.

Siv sat in a thicket at the base of the foothills for several minutes with his mouth open, the ground around him wet with his tears. Eventually, he walked in the direction of the burrow along the edge of the foothills beneath the thickets which remained there. Ilyana and one of Yuryk's guards followed close behind. There were times when they were exposed, but Siv didn't care. His heart no longer pounded nervously in his chest. His tiny paws were numb as he picked his way across the ground. He walked, but it was like he floated. In that place inside himself where, only moments ago, he had felt fear and hope in equal measure, now there was only a deep emptiness.

Before he turned the corner to the safety of the burrow, he looked back one last time. His tear sacs filled with regret and burst onto the ashen wasteland one more time as he looked upon his fallen brothers and sisters. So many dead on his account. Nearly their entire clan, wiped out. How had his plan gone so horribly wrong?

The Watcher allowed this to happen.

Wern had described Jaerwin well. This was the scene of a madman. Before he could turn away, he noticed a change taking place on the field.

One by one, the bodies were disappearing.

Escape

Throughout the night, survivors filtered into the burrow in small groups. Some had escaped Laguznal's flame by running toward Svernos and following its mountain shadow back to the burrow, while others had followed the foothills route Siv had taken.

The numbers were dismal. The dragon had reduced the clan to a fraction of its former size. What had been close to a thousand was now at seventy-two, after an official count was taken in the Council Chamber the following morning. Siv fully expected retribution for the failure. He spoke plainly on accepting responsibility for the plan, and he expected Yuryk to capitalize on the opportunity to pinpoint the blame to him.

Whether he was sent to the Room Below or executed, he would take his punishment without complaint. There was no benevolent creator watching over them. He knew that now. Even though he'd lost much of his family and himself in the process, at least he could take solace in the truth. Wern had been right to despair. The good feelings, the hopefulness he had received from Jaerwin was all just trickery. His God was no more than a self-indulgent human that had somehow found a god-like power. But for all his might, he was just one of those men that had come at them with spears and deadly projectile weapons. Jaerwin's weapon was deceit. That was far worse. The humans could tear at his flesh with their weapons, but Jaerwin had torn him apart from the inside.

To Siv's surprise, at the Council meeting Yuryk and the others made it clear that they had no intention of punishing the seer. The idea was not even considered. Siv didn't get as much relief from this as he should have, for he was over-whelmed with guilt. It seemed, however, that the clan was worn down and dying. There was no anger, no fight in any of them. Despite the horrific turn of his last plan, the clan still looked to Siv as seer.

"We were so close," Ilyana said. "The falls were right there. Strigo made it. I saw him." Ilyana's comment was a small sunbeam in a world with no light. Though it hardly made up for the mass casualties, the operation hadn't been a total failure, after all.

Strigo did make it with the Tome. I saw him too.

Had he flown to the top as his eagle? His aviary form was large enough to clutch the Tome in its talons. He could be up there waiting for them now...

"We can't go back out there," said one vilskje. "Not after what happened. We have to stay here and just figure a way to sneak in food."

"You'd have us live in fear... forever?" Ilyana said with her strongest patronizing tone. "You want us to sneak around every day just to survive? I can see why you are not seer."

"Thank you, but that's enough, Ilyana," Siv said. "He is right to express this concern after what just happened." He turned to the room at large. "You all are. I've gotten nearly our entire clan killed. I've failed you."

Yuryk stood from Wern's engravement in the floor and stepped forward. "You were right, Seer. If we stayed here, it would have meant a slow death for us all by starvation. We had to do *something*. We had a miserable result, but your advice was keen. If anything, I am more now than ever eager to leave this dragon in our history. Let us go and you may scribble him into your Tome."

"How?" said an elder. "We tried once and look what happened. You'd have us go about it again?

A scout, one of three remaining, entered the chamber and spoke. "Zurt is alive! He was hiding in a dip in the valley through the night. He's coming to join us now."

The crowd roared in applause. Zurt and Delagria were two of the most beloved elders in the clan and their fame had only grown after their sacrifices. Zurt entered the room with his head down, both tear sacs full. His posture confirmed what everyone had already suspected—Delagria had been killed.

"There is another way, I think," said Siv, surprising even himself with his sudden speech. Ilyana's reminder of Strigo had given him the smallest sliver of hope. "Strigo made it, so we must go meet him."

"Yes, but how?" said one vilskje.

"We follow the river up along the foothills, again as our rodents. Only this time, we go in two's, not all at once. The first pair leaves and one hour later the next one, and so on. If Laguznal finds us, we jump into the river and ride the current down. Flames are far less effective under water."

"There's no way I'm going back out there," said another vilskje.

Zurt made his way beside Yuryk, drawing many eyes. He raised a hand to get everyone's attention. "Please, my Delagria sacrificed herself for our clan. Don't let her deed be in vain. We mustn't give up. This is what she would want as well."

"We will take a vote," said Yuryk. "All in favor of staying here and trying to survive, raise a claw!" Several vilskje arms went up. "Now, those in favor of following the river north and escaping over the falls, raise a claw!" Many more arms went up. "Then, it is settled. Seer, when do we depart?"

Siv came to stand beside Yuryk. "I see no reason to wait. We will go in pairs—one with avian ability and the other not. Bird will carry rodent to the top of Tevryk Falls. Fly in the space *behind* the falls to avoid being seen by the dragon! Remember, if you are spotted, you will ruin the plan for everyone. The first pair leaves in one hour."

Laguznal circled above as the vilskje made their second attempt at escaping the vale, but their small numbers didn't attract the dragon's attention and their new route wasn't a focus of its gaze. The hardest part was at the falls, where one rodent would shift to a bird, clutching its companion in its talons and flying unseen behind the waterfall. Near the top, it would rotate outside the falls and fly over the top to safety.

Thirty-six hours later, the entire clan had made it safely behind the falls, stunned at just how seamlessly the plan had worked. They looked at Siv with newfound admiration. Siv looked out over Windlyn Vale—his home for the many centuries of his life. To the south, Laguznal let out the occasional scream, but the reptile's attention didn't turn their way. Siv began to consider that he had been wrong about the Watcher. Jaerwin had come through at the end. Perhaps he didn't have as much control as Siv assumed he did.

Delagria, may the Watcher bless you. By the light, we will honor you in our new home.

Strigo met Siv at the top, delivering him the Great Tome. Siv confirmed the dragon blood was still in there, patting the stalwart on the back and reminding him of his promise to include him in council decisions. It was a promise he intended to deliver on. Siv fell back to huddle beside Ilyana behind the crest at the top of the falls, claws resting on one another. It was their haven for now. A warmth spread inside Siv's chest and he closed his eyes.

They had made it.

SHIPS

After several hours, the vilskje finally accepted the dragon wouldn't follow them over the falls, and one by one they fell asleep.

But Siv stayed up the full night, not with worry, but with wonder. After surviving the dragon and witnessing his eager apprentice, Atul, savagely killed, what worse could the path forward bring? What could be worse than what Laguznal had done to their clan? Nothing.

Nothing could surpass that sadness. The burning of the vilskje and humans, who came at them likely through misunderstanding. Nothing could be worse than watching the poor, pleading boy burn, all alone in their homeland after they had turned him away. Nothing was worse than the atrocity of watching his lifeless, charred body floating away, down the Zaqar river to the sea, to be consumed by sharks. They could have saved him with a mere sliver of grace. Nothing, by far, was worse than the hundreds of vilskje that were burned alive in the grass of their own homeland.

But that was all behind them.

Now, we've begun our exodus.

The best thing of all, Siv realized, wasn't that they had made it there safely. It was the beauty of Delagria's sacrifice. They would have to go on with only a fondness and love in their heart for that unexpected deed by the eldest common blood of their clan. They were the unheralded. The first of the lie that was the so-called "common creation."

It was a stark reminder of the extent of the fabrication. For, aside from Atul, the greatest vilskje he had known were of that label. Not only Delagria and Zurt, but also Ilyana, his dearest surviving friend.

Yuryk's voice came from the bottom of a slope behind the falls. "Rise, my clan. It's time we leave this place."

The clan stirred, a tangle of lean insectile appendages and tiny black eyes beneath the bright morning sun.

"We rest too close to the dragon," Yuryk continued.

They stumbled to their feet, comforted that the stone crest protruding from the top of the cliff hid them. Just ahead, a river ran to the edge and spilled to the falls, becoming the mouth of the Zaqar river. They had never seen this part of the river before. It was beyond the borders of their realm. Beyond the supposed edge of the world.

"Yuryk is right," said Siv, addressing the clan. "We should continue north, away from the dragon. It has no reason to come this way, and we must give it no reason to."

Siv walked slowly down the slope, taking in the land before him. Just how small had been their part of the world? While the river continued upstream along a higher path in the distance, the view cut off by trees, a separate lower path forked to the east. This lower landscape was more open, showing a forest in the far distance, a vast mountain, and, off in a cove, floating structures on the surface of the sea.

Ilyana walked up beside him, stretching. "What are those?" She pointed to the floating structures.

"Ships," Siv said. "Vessels that sail over the water. It appears we haven't left the humans behind after all."

The realization should have given him worry, but it didn't. He had peace of mind in this new place. This is where they were supposed to be.

"We must learn to coexist, I think. I wonder why none of these ships sailed into Windlyn Vale."

Siv shrugged. "Perhaps it's more of Jaerwin's doing."

"One day, I should like to sail on one," Ilyana said.

"I would go alongside you." He stopped, turning to face her.

She smiled and met his gaze.

The clan followed the slope, leaving Windlyn Vale behind. Yuryk must have seen the ships, yet he said nothing. Likely, he was as fascinated as the rest of them. The world was not the small place they had thought it was. Eventually, though, the reality set in of this new, scary world without their burrow.

"What do we do now?" asked one of the vilskje in the back.

"We'll find a new home," Siv said. "We won't look back. Only to the future."

"A new burrow," Yuryk said, in rare agreement. "With tunnels and chambers like we are used to. We'll start at the mountains up ahead. There may be caves there."

"And if we don't find any?" asked another.

"Then we take to the sea," said Ilyana, and she took Siv's claw firmly in her own.

EPILOGUE

Back in his Fallbright lab, Drexel ran dreg root through the fine chopper, wrinkling his nose at the swamp smell. The roots looked unsavory, like nose hairs freshly plucked from a giant, but they smelled even worse. He pulled a flask from a shelf and uncorked it, averting his nose. He whirled his nimble hand around to allow the mist to trail off into the air. From another shelf he grabbed an open bottle of spring water. With precision, he mixed one quarter goblet of dreg root dust, with a full swig of spring water, adding four drops of intensifier to the beaker. He swirled it around, watching the mixture morph into various shades of green until it settled into just the right hue.

Normally, he adored this process, his mind on his cash-dragon, Laguznal, and the future profits his sleeping injections would allow. But several days ago, something had changed. He'd woken in the middle of the night, sweating, his gut twisting like a gnarled branch. His mind had gone immediately to the abyss dragon, but he had reached for another conclusion. For denial is the one trait that pixies exhibit with greater magnitude than mischief, when the need presents itself.

He could not accept that the dragon had woken up. It simply could not be. And so, he had proceeded as normal, his gut tied in an infernal knot. His throat dry and his eyes bloodshot. The chorus was worried about him, being already well-known as a troublemaker in Fallbright, but he assured them all was well. Wonderful even.

But denial has its limits and he'd reached his breaking point. The awful feeling hadn't gone away. It had festered. The feeling of future losses. Of failure.

He had to know.

Beaker firmly in hand, Drexel bolted from his lab, sprang over the hill and across the bridge which ran over the babbling brook at the center of their village. He sprinted down the cobbled path, ignoring glances from other Fallbright pixies until he burst through the door of his ornate home, built atop the tombs of ancient, long-forgotten men. A hallway and stair climb later, he came to the room which held the magical device he was seeking.

The dragon finder.

He had intentionally avoided this room—while telling himself that was not at all the case—since that first twist in his gut. Since that first sweaty night. But, deep inside, he had known the truth. One glance at the device told him all he needed to know. There was a red dot on the map symbolizing a certain dragon hundreds of miles away. Now, for the first time since he'd started his blood-business, the dot was moving.

Drexel's body shook, his blood-shot eyes trembled, his

ears twitched. His arm exploded forward, launching the dreg root mixture into the far stone wall, smashing the beaker and draining its contents over his fine furnishings. He screamed an animal scream, loud enough that the dead men in the tomb below his home may even have heard it. If they had, they might have chosen to remain dead rather than meet him.

Several minutes later, Drexel regained his bearings. He stood in the same spot, his body drenched in sweat. He spun his dragon finder around so he would not see its infuriating information again. Then he walked slowly and calmly from the room and up another flight of stairs until he reached his pixie armory. He snapped his fingers, sending a round sharpening stone spinning on its own. Then, he selected two of the finest, cruelly twisted daggers from his display case and sat down on the cushioned bench. He held the blades up to the stone, sending sparks flying as they sharpened to razor thin edges.

"Siv, you shifty bastard," Drexel fumed, grinding his teeth until his jaw was sore. "What a mistake you have made."

THE STORY CONTINUES...

We've not seen the last of Siv, Drexel, Ilyana, or the vilskje. The story continues in Grave Covenant, Book One of the upcoming Projectionists Series. See what happens when the remaining clan attempts to integrate into human society. Join The Tobias Youngblood Newsletter to receive updates on the release.

In addition, members will get free exclusive content as it is released, special offers, and more.

It's completely free to sign up and you'll never be spammed by me. You can opt out at any time.

Sign up at www.tobiasyoungblood.com

Acknowledgments

Thank you to Landen for listening to my crazy ideas and inspiring me with his own creative mind. Thank you to Lyra for lifting me every day with her energy and beautiful free spirit. Thank you to Dawn for the love and loyalty through the years. Thank you to my family and to Luna, for keeping my feet warm while I write.

Thank you to the many critique partners and beta-readers in and out of SFFWHR. Your input was valuable and instrumental.

And thanks, most of all, to you for reading Windlyn Vale. I hope you enjoyed it.

About the Author

Tobias Youngblood lives in Coastal Virginia, where he grew up reading fantasy, sci-fi, and horror. Early influences include J.R.R. Tolkien, Roald Dahl, Clive Barker, and Ray Bradbury among countless others. For as long as he can remember, Tobias dreamed of being an author. But, somehow, his dream was neglected, and it became lost to the doldrums of the real world.

Years later, he stumbled upon it in the back crease of a desolate drawer. A shrunken, resentful thing, it was yet beautiful as it gasped for what might have been its last breath. Sad, but inspired, Tobias gently carried it to the hearth where the firelight has since nurtured it.

Tobias Youngblood is the author of Windlyn Vale, a fantasy novella and prequel to the upcoming Projectionists trilogy, set to release in 2023.